# THE PRIEST'S FIRE

# THE PRIEST'S FIRE

## HEINOUS CRIMES UNIT™ BOOK TWO

DANIEL SCOTT

MARLOWE & VANE

Copyright © 2017, 2022 Daniel Scott & David Beers
Cover Art by Jake @ J Caleb Design
http://jcalebdesign.com / jcalebdesign@gmail.com
Cover copyright © Marlow & Vane

Published by Marlowe & Vane
an imprint of LMBPN Publishing
PMB 196, 2540 South Maryland Pkwy
Las Vegas, NV 89109

Previously Published as *The Priest*
Version 1.01, January 2023
ebook ISBN: 979-8-88541-371-8
Print ISBN: 979-8-88541-896-6

# THE PRIEST'S FIRE TEAM

**Thanks to our JIT Readers**

David Laughlin
Kelly O'Donnell
Daphne Reilly
John Ashmore
Marty French
Alison Kelly

**Editor**

Natale Wynne-Morril

# THE BOOK OF GENESIS

# CHAPTER ONE

Lucy Speckle stared at the television. Her attention focused entirely on it, not noticing the small tics that broke out across her face from time to time. The people around her didn't notice either, but it wasn't because they were focused on the TV like Lucy. They had…other issues.

"We are here today to commemorate an FBI agent whose name many of you probably already know. His accomplishments are nearly legendary, and we are all lucky to have him helping keep our citizens safe. We'd like to present Luke Titan with our highest award."

Lucy didn't know the man speaking and she didn't care about him either. He was *nonessential.* Lucy believed heavily in the essential and the nonessential. Anything that didn't fit into the first bucket could be discarded without further thought, and in Lucy's mind, there was only a single *essential* guiding force: the one true God of Abraham and Isaac.

Yet, despite the *non-essentialness* of the man speaking, she couldn't pull herself away from the screen. However, she wasn't looking at *him*, or the person he appeared to be speaking *about*.

Lucy's stare fixed on someone on the back left. His hands were folded in front of him, and he looked uncomfortable in his suit and tie. To Lucy Speckle, it was clear he didn't want to be on stage.

"Who is that?" Lucy asked, her voice snapping through the room's silence—her normal stutter missing.

"Lucy, please stay calm," someone nonessential said from her side.

For the most part, all the people working here were nonessential. They didn't serve God, but the government, an evil thing that Lucy had no time for. She knew God would get her out of this wretched place sooner or later. He had put her here for a reason. Even if she didn't understand it yet, she trusted Him implicitly.

Staring at the television screen, she thought perhaps she'd found the reason. The man standing onstage, to the left.

How long had the preacher spoken about this moment? For how many years had her and Daddy—and Momma, to a far lesser degree—prayed for worthiness? To be shown exactly what Lucy now saw?

"Who is that?" She stood, ignoring the orderly next to her, and walked to the television, placing her hand directly on the man. "Who is he?" She looked around the room, but she saw only blank faces. "What is his *name*?"

Lucy was growing angry at these people, the fact that no one would answer her.

"His name is Christian Windsor," another orderly said. Three more nonessentials had come into the room, ready to calm Lucy Speckle if she couldn't do it herself. "He's an FBI agent."

There, that was all she needed. Lucy stepped a few feet back from the television and stared at Christian Windsor. Even the name seemed...

*Godly.*

Her right eyebrow twitched, and her head jerked down slightly before regaining its usual place. Lucy didn't notice.

She stared at the screen for a long time, until the ceremony ended and the next show started. Only then did she break her concentration.

Lucy walked to a corner in the large room and found a chair away from everyone else. She sat and thought about the man on TV.

---

The next few weeks were turbulent for Lucy. She often found herself angry at those around her, which meant she ended up in one of those jackets that wouldn't let her move. They called it a straitjacket. She called it "fucking bullshit," one of the few times Lucy Speckle used such language, and she spat at the orderlies who put it on her.

God didn't like curse words. Daddy had used them when he was mad, although he always repented.

They were nonessentials, but she still couldn't help the anger she felt toward them. She shouldn't be in here, not with all the rest of these crazies. She didn't know how long she had been here. She hadn't been good at keeping up with time since Daddy died, but now that she had seen Christian Windsor she knew she'd been here *too* long.

No one ever visited her, and that was more than fine. She didn't want to talk with anyone. Not her family, who had pretty much disowned Daddy decades ago. Lucy never had any friends. She didn't need any besides God, and He was always with her.

Those weeks were awful, especially when she was locked away inside the straitjacket. She felt God trying to speak, but she couldn't hear Him well inside this place. It was like the walls were built with a material that kept God out.

Lucy knew that couldn't possibly be true, that the God of Abraham and Isaac did whatever He wanted when He wanted. Perhaps the walls simply interfered with *her* ability to hear Him.

Yes. That made more sense.

Either way, the result was the same. Lucy knew that the person she had seen on the television screen— *Christian Windsor*—was the one she, Daddy, and the whole church had been searching for, but she wanted more confirmation.

Lucy quit fighting the orderlies and doctors who came around. Just as she had realized years ago how nonessential the kids mocking her at school were, she understood that fighting these nonessentials was keeping God at bay. So, she lay down on her bed and quit caring about this ephemeral world, which was only a test from God, and one she had to rise above.

She urinated and defecated on herself during this time. Her eyes never left the ceiling. She didn't move at all when the orderlies came to change her clothes. She made her arms and legs pliable as they undressed and redressed her.

Only a few more hours would pass before more bodily functions occurred, and the orderlies had to do it all again.

She didn't care. Truthfully, she didn't even notice. Lucy had gone to God. For once, she was able to do it without the instruments Daddy had given her.

*God* was talking to *her*.

In the end, it was glorious, Lucy finally understood Daddy hadn't been lying all those years. They had been chosen, even if Daddy wasn't here to see it. The nonessential fell away for good, leaving only room for the essential.

*That* was Christian Windsor. *He* was what God wanted for Lucy Speckle. What this whole hellish world had been about.

To prepare her for him—*God's sword*.

# CHAPTER TWO

*Two Years Later*

"I'm hungry," Christian said.

"When are you not?" Tommy Phillips, one of Christian's partners at the FBI, asked.

"You're disgusting," Luke Titan, the third in the trio, said.

The three of them were staring at a body. Christian was used to such comments from the other two. He couldn't help it when he got hungry. Plus, it *was* lunchtime.

"We shouldn't be here anyway. These guys are just lazy." Christian saw Tommy shaking his head, and quickly realized his snafu in talking about the police officers who had called them down here since they happened to still be in the room.

Christian looked up from the body. "I'm sorry. I have a problem filtering when I'm hungry."

The three cops in front of him stared, not kindly. None said a word.

Christian looked back down at the body, determined to keep his mouth shut for the rest of this endeavor.

Luke turned on the charm. "I'm sorry about Agent Windsor. He's … Well, he operates a bit differently. Saying that, while I don't agree with his sentiment, I don't think this is a case our unit would take."

*Of course it isn't*, Christian thought. The body in front of them had clearly been killed by gang members. They had cut the tongue out, so the police immediately wanted to classify it as a pathological crime that would fall under the FBI's purview. Most of the time, the cops simply didn't want to deal with the paperwork, so they tried to shove things off on Christian's unit.

"Thanks for your time," Tommy said. "If you need anything from us, please don't hesitate to call."

After the perfunctory handshakes, which Christian was blessedly left out of, the three of them left the room and walked upstairs.

"Well, that was nice of you, Christian," Luke said, smiling as they exited the morgue. "You just keep making friends."

"If you two would have simply taken me to lunch, I wouldn't have said anything else."

"I'm not doing subs," Tommy said. "It'll be the fourth time this week. Luke, what do you want?"

"I'm indifferent."

"Damn it," Tommy said. He looked at Christian. "No subs. Pick something else."

"Chinese?"

"Fine."

The three of them got into their car and pulled out of

the parking lot. They didn't spend many days like this, heading to police stations or morgues where the crimes committed had nothing to do with their division, but they did it more than any of them wanted to.

Two years had passed since the Surgeon had made national news. Christian always thought of him as Bradley Brown. Even though Luke had ended up saving Tommy and Christian by putting a bullet through Bradley's face, Christian felt a sense of sorrow for the man. He was dead and his eyeless mother was in a state-run home now.

Tommy and Luke could discount Bradley's early life, before he began his murder spree, but Christian couldn't. He had seen what happened to turn a young kid into such a horrible monster.

The cases they worked on now were mostly dead ends, one-time murders. They hadn't found any cults, serial killers, or many truly crazy people in the past two years. There had been a few up north, and a few out west, but the southeast region had been relatively quiet.

"Are either of you getting bored?"

He saw Luke's small grin. He automatically knew what Christian was asking about. Their connection had grown stronger over the past two years. It was their intelligence. Both of them had minds that maneuvered at ferocious speeds that most others couldn't even imagine.

The suspicions Christian had about Luke two years ago, that he might have been a murderer, never crossed his mind anymore. It was the only time in Christian's twenty-eight years that his mind had missed something. Bradley Brown's obsession with Luke had driven Christian's brain to make connections that didn't exist.

"Bored of what?" Tommy asked.

"Of the job."

"Ready to transfer out?" Tommy asked.

The thought had never occurred to Christian. He couldn't imagine life without the two people in the front seats, any more than he could imagine life without his mother or his psychiatrist. These two were his family, his friends, and Christian couldn't fathom replacing them.

"No. Why would I do that?"

"You know that at some point we will all leave this division, right?" Luke said. "It's amazing that the three of us are still here after two years."

"The Director is pressuring Luke right now to take another position."

"Waverly?" Christian asked.

"Yes, sir. He wants Luke to take over the west coast, dealing with violent crimes that cross state lines. Primarily gang-related offenses."

Christian was stunned. Somehow, despite all his intelligence, he hadn't considered that they might go their separate ways. "Are you going to take it?"

"No, I don't think so."

"Luke is an idiot, if you haven't noticed," Tommy said. "However, he may be the only person in the FBI who can pass up an opportunity like that and not have to worry. They'll always be trying to move him up the ranks, which gives him leeway to accept what he wants."

"So when something better comes for you, you'll jump ship?" Christian said.

"Jump ship?" Tommy said. "You know we get a pension? And it's based on how high our salary is when we retire. I want some pretty big paychecks when I retire. You should too."

Christian fell silent.

He'd originally thought he would stay with the FBI for ten years or so and then use his dual doctorates for other endeavors. He hadn't considered that plan in years, though. Somehow, in his mind, he figured the three of them would ride this thing out until… Until what? Until they died or retired?

"Hey," Tommy said. "No one's leaving to go anywhere yet. And, when we do, it's not like we can't still see each other. Don't worry about it. Nothing's happened, and nothing's going to happen for the foreseeable future."

Telling Christian not to worry about something was like telling an alcoholic to put down his drink, and everyone in the car knew it.

---

Luke watched Christian poke a fork into his fried rice. He refused to eat with chopsticks, saying they were the largest form of idiocy he could imagine.

"If an alien species comes down and finds us using two sticks to eat our food, they'll kill us on general principle."

Luke hated the food in these places—in *all* the places that Tommy and Christian chose to eat. He came and he ate with them because he was concerned only with the long term. He had always thought that way, but now it was more important than ever.

He knew why Christian wasn't eating. It was because the boy was upset about the possibility of the band breaking up. His normally prodigious appetite was stunted while he dwelled on it.

Luke wasn't going to let the band go anywhere, even if he couldn't tell Christian that. Luke had turned down the position he was offered for that exact reason. It wasn't the first offer Waverly had presented to him, and it wouldn't be the last. Luke Titan was widely viewed as the most talented FBI agent in the entire organization. Tommy was right. If anyone else had turned down such an offer, their career would be dead in the water. More offers would come for Luke…although, he didn't care in the slightest.

This team, this band, was what mattered to him. But for very different reasons than it did to Christian.

Two years had passed for Luke without sufficient opportunity to continue his plans. The crimes they investigated simply weren't *big* enough. There had been no cases on a scale that would create the confusion and chaos he desired. Bradley Brown had almost been large enough, but in the end, Luke had relented and killed the psychopath, saving the people he had set up in the first place.

He'd received his medal and the gratitude of the FBI, even though Christian Windsor and Tommy Phillips had been tied up in Bradley Brown's house *because* of him.

"You're really worrying about what I said in the car, aren't you?" Tommy asked.

"Yes," Christian said.

"Why, man? I just told you no one is going anywhere."

"But you will, eventually."

"But when? We don't know, so why worry about it?" Tommy asked.

Christian didn't respond. Luke took a bite of his food,

not looking at the boy. He still thought of him like that, as a *boy*. Admittedly, he felt a certain fondness for him. Perhaps Christian and Tommy were right and maybe Luke had been waiting too long. His chaos could start at any time.

Was he enjoying this? Their company? In some way, perhaps yes, but that didn't mean one could deny their purpose.

Yes. Maybe it was time to begin.

---

"How are you feeling today?" Luke asked.

Veronica Lopez thought it odd how easily she'd switched from calling him Dr. Titan to Luke over the past two years. Odd, because this had begun as strictly profes-sional, but now she considered him a friend. Maybe it shouldn't seem odd. Wasn't that what always happened when you were around someone long enough? She'd seen Luke every month over the past two years. Her therapy had begun with the Bradley Brown incident, but it had expanded much further.

"I'm doing okay, I guess. Stress from work."

"What kind of stress?"

They were sitting in Luke's spacious living room. He was in a large, leather chair, and she was on the couch catty-corner to it. The man knew how to decorate, that was obvious. The couch felt like clouds beneath her and it never ceased to amaze. She'd always wanted to ask him how much it cost but never did.

"I don't know what I'm going to write next," she said, answering his question.

"Well, we could always arrange to have another killer trap you," Luke suggested with a slight smirk.

"Hard pass." She was okay with his jokes now that she understood his personality. Luke saw everything in a different light. Some people wore dark sunglasses and others wore rose-colored ones, with most switching between the two depending on the situation. Luke saw the world with perfect, bright clarity—the sun's light illuminating everything. It gave him an ability to dismiss emotions, Veronica supposed, to a large degree. It also made him effective as a therapist. "You still haven't picked up any other patients?"

"No. I don't have enough time. You're the only woman in my life, Veronica." Still smiling, he changed the subject. "Have you thought about going back to the book on the Sphere?"

The Sphere. The book that had led her to all of this, to Luke Titan and his world. To Christian Windsor, Tommy Phillips, and ending with Bradley-Fucking-Brown.

"It's dead. They stopped working on it." The Sphere had been Luke Titan's invention back when he was in academia, before switching careers to the FBI. It was an odd career path. Psychiatrist, astrophysicist, and finally Special Agent. "You were the engine that kept it moving."

"You could write about that. I always love the good press."

"You could start working on it again. That would give me something to write on."

"Maybe I will one day. Not today, though," Luke said.

They sat quietly for a few seconds. Luke did this often, letting the silence dominate until she was forced to speak.

"I've got to write something. I just don't know what."

"Well, what are your talents?"

"What do you mean?" she said.

"What are you good at?"

"Writing."

"And what are you good at writing about?" Luke asked.

Veronica thought for a second. "Investigative journalism. I'm good at portraying people in a way that makes others understand them."

Luke nodded. "Yes, that's right. People are complex. We have emotions running through us constantly, dominating our thoughts all day long. Animals do the same, but they lack the multitude of thoughts. Theirs are simple, so it's easier to understand them. You have a talent that allows people to understand the essence of others. To boil away all the extraneous thoughts, so the masses can see inside someone. *The Surgeon* sold so well, not because you wrote about your experiences of being kidnapped and tortured. It certainly wasn't because you wrote about me. The book sold because you explained Bradley Brown's past in a way that made people understand him, even though he was a monster. *That's* what people want. Do it again."

"It's that easy, huh? Just simply pick a man off the street and start writing about him. That'll be a bestseller, I'm sure."

Luke smiled again. "Well, there are interesting people out there, many of them right around you."

"Name one."

"Christian Windsor."

Veronica's head jerked backward at the name. At one point, they had discussed Christian frequently during therapy. How could they not? He was an intricate part of the whole Bradley Brown horror show, and Veronica had recruited Christian's help to prove *Luke* was a murderer. All of that was in the past now. Silly notions.

"What would I focus on if I wrote about him? He's a savant, but he hasn't done anything yet."

"He will, though. I can promise that."

"The problem is, Luke, I can't write about a man before he does something. No one wants a biography about that."

"Do you trust me, Veronica?"

She nodded. She trusted him implicitly, more so than perhaps anyone else in her life.

"Then talk to him. I think you'll find him a subject that the masses will want to learn about."

# CHAPTER THREE

Just as two years passed for the others, they also passed for Lucy Speckle.

She spent those two years becoming a model citizen, so to speak. No more outbursts. No more cursing or spitting. She came to realize that if she was to ever leave this place, all the nonessential things had to become *essential*. She even learned the name of where they kept her.

Greenbriar Lakes.

A great name, despite there not being a lake anywhere around her.

The subtitle, which sat on the sign outside, read, "Where People Come To Recover."

That's what Lucy spent her two years doing, recovering.

Christian Windsor was still out there and God hadn't told her to do anything differently. The plan was clear and so she needed to act as these people wanted her to.

Lucy first worked on controlling her facial tics. The involuntary muscle spasms in her neck caused her head to switch one way and the other, regardless of what was happening around her. She started working on speaking clearly, too, though both were extremely hard.

There had been a time in Lucy's life when she wanted nothing more than to quit stuttering. First in school, and the kids who had never stopped their torture. Her father, too. Sometimes, at night, when Lucy was deep in sleep, she could still see her father's face screaming at her.

*"Stop your stuttering. Stop it, goddamnit!"*

She would cringe and cry, and eventually, Daddy would make her repent for the stuttering. It used to bother her, because when you repent, God was supposed to forgive. God never forgave Lucy, or if he did, he certainly didn't stop the stuttering.

When Daddy died, Lucy quit caring about it. Daddy was the last essential person she knew. However, she needed to at least *appear* to be working on the stutter.

Her review day had finally come, and *this* was why she had worked so hard. A chance to escape and find Christian Windsor.

Lucy was sitting in Dr. Brigham's office. She had even spent the time to learn his first name: John. These things were essential if she was to get out.

"How's it going today, Lucy?"

"Good," she said, fighting the stutter that wanted to come out and turn *good* to *g-g-good*.

Lucy's file was open on Dr. Brigham's desk but she didn't look down at it. It was only essential in that it would decide whether she left this place, but she knew how she acted was also essential. She couldn't pay too much attention to it.

"Today is your review day. You know that, right?"

She nodded. "Yes." Short words helped keep the stuttering at bay.

"I've got to say, Lucy, I've been remarkably impressed with your change in behavior. You attended all your therapy sessions. You have had no angry outbursts. You're even running a Bible study? Is that right?"

Another nod. Lucy kept her hands folded in her lap.

"The state remanded you to us after what happened at the woman's home. We've talked about that day a lot, haven't we?"

"Yes." Of course they did. Lucy hated it when he spoke to her like a child.

"Do you think you'd ever do something like that again, Lucy?"

"No, of cuh-course, not. It was wrong." A stutter. No more. No more. No more.

"Why?"

"Because I hurt people. A lot of them. I-I had no reason to hurt any of them and I know that now. I cuh-can't let my anger out like that. It's not fair to them."

"It's not fair to you, either," Dr. Brigham said.

"I know."

A long moment passed between Lucy and the doctor. He looked at her and she kept her eyes firmly on him. She wouldn't look away because this was perhaps the *most* essential moment. A judgment day, of sorts.

"I feel safe recommending that you are released, Lucy. Congratulations on such a remarkable recovery. I hope you understand how far you've come, and I truly hope you continue down this path you've set yourself on."

Lucy smiled.

---

Going to the woman's home had been, by any measure—including Lucy's—a disaster. Until the end. Then Lucy thought it had turned out quite okay.

She'd gone there after Daddy died, though not immediately. She'd tried to find work in her small southern town, but most people had looked at her as a pariah. After what had happened to her mother, and then the way Daddy died? No one was hiring her.

She even went to the church.

It was a small place, of course. Their religious convictions "wouldn't never appeal to all those uppities," her father had explained.

Pastor Martin had said he was very, very sorry, but the church just couldn't take on anyone else. The budget was too tight as it was, and if he brought someone else on, he wouldn't be able to feed his own family.

He said they'd take up a collection at Sunday service.

He took up the collection, but Lucy never saw a nickel, and how much would she have gotten from the ten people sitting in the pews?

So, Lucy had left and headed to the only real city she knew about, Atlanta. She spent the first year working two or three part-time jobs, but she ran into problems. Lucy's tics and stutters kept her from being able to work most hospitality jobs, and those were the only places hiring someone with only a high school diploma from a town they'd never heard of.

So, eventually, Lucy had ended up in the women's shelter.

She'd hated it from the get-go. She looked around and saw nothing but heathens. People on drugs or alcohol, or having multiple kids out of wedlock. There were classes and therapists and everything else you could imagine. Her father had talked about it all before, the "ills of society" as he termed it. The ills were people that couldn't take care of themselves and relied on drugs or booze to hide their failures from themselves.

"All them city folks gotta do is to turn to the Lord. Once they do that, everythin' else will be just fine."

Lucy tried to preach to them, and when she did, her stutter disappeared. That was the miracle of God. While He may not have helped Lucy when Daddy told her to repent, as soon as she spoke about the Lord, the stutter couldn't be found.

Her preaching went nowhere and she was asked to stop by the staff.

The moment which landed her in Greenbriar Lakes came shortly after that.

She just hadn't been able to take it anymore. Watching the people around her destroy their lives. Smoking their cigarettes. Coming in from their "jobs." Lucy *knew* they'd been at bars talking to men and getting loaded.

Finally, she caught one of the women—her name was lost in the recesses of Lucy's mind if it'd ever been there to begin with—smoking those cigarettes. The body was a temple, the Lord made that clear, and here *she* was just destroying it. Destroying God's work.

Lucy didn't think it was that big of a deal at the time.

Certainly nothing like what God did to Sodom and Gomorrah. She'd grabbed the cigarette from the woman's hand and put it out on her face. The woman had shrieked and jerked back, but the red flesh shone like a tiny sun on her skin where the cigarette burned her.

Lucy had liked the way that felt, and she knew God liked her delivering a bit of justice. If they didn't respect their bodies, why should their flesh continue looking pristine? Well, as pristine as whores and drunks could look.

Lucy had continued walking around the outside, pulling cigarettes from people's hands and simply grinding them out on whatever piece of the smoker she could get to. Hands, foreheads, eyes, mouths. She didn't care.

She went through seven people before the shrieks and cries finally alerted the staff to come and stop Lucy's righteous vengeance.

She struggled hard against the men and women who came for her. Daddy had made sure Lucy was strong, and while the muscle she'd gained back home was lean and thin on her frame, it had never left. She punched, kicked, bit, and raked her nails every which way.

Eventually, they'd brought her down to the ground. Her nose and mouth were bleeding, but she'd felt good for the first time in a long time.

Daddy had told her that God was just, but he was also cruel to those who disregarded His laws.

Lucy would never be the Lord's sword, but she'd done something good that day.

The courts had looked at it differently. Lucy had listened to the nonessentials talk about her without saying a word. She had provided no defense, and the court had found her incapable of determining right from wrong—a rarity, as Lucy later found out—and they'd remanded her to Greenbriar Lakes with no stated return-to-society date.

Lucy *knew* right from wrong.

It was the world that didn't understand the difference.

---

Lucy quickly found out that being released from Greenbriar Lakes didn't mean complete freedom. She went to what was termed a halfway house, and if God had never tested her before, he was doing so now.

This place was much worse than the women's shelter, but Lucy had to remember her goal. She had an important purpose, to usher in the Lord's sword.

The halfway house got her a job as a maid at a local hotel. She went to it dutifully every day, speaking to almost no one. Her bosses stayed away for the most part, besides barking orders from time to time about something that needed cleaning.

Lucy didn't mind the work. She worked alone, which she preferred. She folded towels, cleaned rooms, picked up used condoms and threw them away, and scraped shit off the inside of toilets. Everything that no one else in this horrible world wanted to do.

But she did it because this wasn't the end for her. It was the beginning.

They allowed her to use the Internet at the halfway house. It took some time at first to learn how to use computers, and then the Internet. Lucy wasn't slow by any means, but her life hadn't been cursed with such sophisticated technologies. Daddy always said they were the Devil's tool, and from what she found on them, she agreed.

For her purposes, it wasn't essential that she know everything about the computer. She had to use something called a search engine. She needed Christian Windsor's name, which she had and would never, ever forget. Then she needed time.

For a solid month, Lucy spent two hours each night on one of the computers the halfway house provided. Sometimes people asked her to get up so that they could use it, and while Lucy wanted to scrape her nails down their faces until their skin fell away, leaving only a bloody mass of meat looking back at her, she acquiesced and gave up the station. It was essential that she stay out of Greenbriar forever.

God was speaking to her more now, which was great.

She heard him loudest when looking at pictures of Christian Windsor. Lucy couldn't print them out and take them to her room like she wanted. That would have been noticed by the nameless staff who walked the halls. She could only look at them on the computer, but when she did, God spoke.

The man was beautiful. Lucy found herself attracted to him in a way that she hadn't felt for anyone before. Sometimes a stirring even happened in her naughty parts, but she was careful not to act on that. Daddy had made it well known that the naughty parts were for excreting waste only, not anything pleasurable. Pleasure wasn't what God wanted for his children.

The human species was too sinful to make it to heaven by indulging in mindless pleasure.

She asked her father once why God made men and women feel for each other. The answer had been obvious, and she was chastised harshly for not seeing it first. The Devil put those feelings there. They had nothing to do with God or His Holiness.

She knew when she met Christian, she could never express those naughty thoughts. God's plans for *him* were much greater than even those he had for Lucy. She wouldn't sully that, not for anything in the world.

It took two months to gather the information she needed.

Then God's work could finally begin.

------

The longer Lucy stayed at the halfway house, the more freedoms they gave her. She was now able to go out one night a week, from 5:00 PM to 10:00 PM. She was very careful to make sure she left on time and returned on time, never once going outside of the designated intervals.

Being careful was essential, especially right now.

Daddy's car had still been parked at the church, even after three years. Pastor Martin said no one had used it and they were just waiting for her to come to pick it up. Lucy didn't believe much of what Pastor Martin said, and he charged her a hefty hundred dollars to bring it to her, but in the end, she got the old car.

So, she did what anyone with an immense endeavor would do. She began practicing.

Lucy knew the routes to take, knew the time necessary to get where she needed to go and then return. She traveled them over the next few months, once each week, learning everything about the back roads, highways, turns, and stop lights.

Finally, she showed up at the state home where Mrs. Brown lived. Bradley Brown's mother, the person who spawned the heathen who had nearly killed Christian. Lucy signed in, having researched extensively what was needed to see someone at the residence. Apparently, nothing more than an ID.

She looked at the blind woman for the first time, hate growing in her heart like a black cloud. This woman had given birth to something almost like Satan. This woman had created a creature that nearly destroyed God's miraculous plan.

"Who are you?" the woman asked.

"M-m-my name is Lucy."

"Why are you here? I don't know you."

The woman wore sunglasses, but Lucy knew underneath those glasses were two dark holes where her son had scooped out her eyeballs.

"I w-w-wanted to come say hi."

"Well, hi," the old woman said.

Lucy made small talk for another hour and then left, barely able to contain her rage. It was, of course, essential that she did.

When she returned to the halfway house, Lucy understood with certainty that God was directing her path. It would be easy to do what was needed.

# CHAPTER FOUR

*One Month Later*

Christian still couldn't shake what Tommy had told him.

Everyone was going to leave him, eventually. That made him think about his mom. He knew factually that she would die one day, but he had always avoided the knowledge as if it were a dead body carrying the plague. He never let it enter his thoughts, not even in his mental mansion where he kept everything he encountered.

"Why does it bother you so much?" Melissa, his psychiatrist, asked.

He sat in her office, having scheduled an emergency appointment the day before as soon as he'd left Tommy and Luke. He needed to talk to someone about this.

"Because I've built my *life* around them. Around my mother. If they leave, what will I have left?"

He stared out the window behind her as he always did when he spoke about something difficult to acknowledge.

"One day you'll die too, Christian, and you'll leave people that have built their life around you."

"No one has built their life around me."

"No?" Melissa said. "What about your mother? She's spent her entire existence serving you, helping you become someone courageous, someone she can be proud of."

"*I* won't leave *her*. She's going to leave me. She's going to *die!*" He shouted the last word and immediately fell silent.

"Tommy said that no one was taking another job right now, correct?"

He nodded.

"Then you're worrying about something that will happen in the future. You could worry about any number of things that *will* happen, but it's not going to change anything."

"You're useless," he said. "You're just trying to logic away what I'm feeling."

"I'm not. I'm trying to make you see that thinking like this isn't healthy. Have you talked to either of them about this? Or your mom?"

"A little today, but I just couldn't… I couldn't believe it."

"Don't you feel that's a bit naive, Christian?"

"Is our time up yet?" he asked.

"It is if you want it to be."

"Good. This has been less than helpful."

Christian stood and left the room without saying anything else. As soon as Melissa's office door closed, the guilt set in. He shouldn't have acted like that. Not to her. She was as much a part of him as the other three, and he had just treated her badly because she didn't agree with him.

Christian wanted to go back in and apologize, but he felt too embarrassed.

He left the office and headed home. It was Saturday, yet another reason he should feel bad for how he treated Melissa. She often set up special times for him, and she had this morning.

His Uber pulled up to his house and Christian handed the driver a five-dollar bill. He had watched an exposé on ride-share drivers a few months back and was disgusted by how much their wages had been cut. So now he tipped the five, and he kept telling Tommy to do the same.

"You don't quit, do you?" Tommy had said last week. "You will literally keep pestering me until I sign my goddamn 401k over to these Uber drivers, won't you?"

"Five dollars would be a start," Christian said.

*You treat your drivers better than your therapist*, he thought as he stepped from the car.

He froze to the spot as the car pulled away.

A box sat in front of his house. He'd bought the house three months ago. His mom had told him that he was burning money living in the apartment, and a home was a smart investment. He knew she was right, so he'd found one that fit comfortably within his budget. Mom had been right on another note, too. It felt like *home*. He was in love with it.

However, he rarely received much mail. He hadn't ordered anything, that was for sure. Christian spent most of his disposable income at Subway, with the rest going to Netflix, movies he rented, and Uber.

Still, the box was there, and Christian stood thirty feet off, staring at it for a long moment.

He walked up his driveway to the front door and stopped when he reached the cardboard box. The tape was wrapped around the top, securing whatever was inside. Christian didn't see any postage anywhere. No UPS stickers or anything else.

"I don't like this."

He squatted down, scared to touch it. This felt wrong, and Christian always trusted his mind. It was capable of fearsome quantitative feats, but what separated him from many other highly functioning autistics was his emotional capacity. He couldn't express his own emotions well, or rather, he expressed them with no filter, but he understood the world around him on levels that others could only grasp at.

And this didn't feel *right*.

He wasn't bringing the box inside his house.

Christian unlocked the front door, went to the kitchen, and grabbed a knife. He brought it back out to the front stoop and carefully cut the box open. The flaps stayed closed, still hiding the contents of the package.

*Don't open this,* he thought. *Call Tommy.*

He called Tommy when he was scared. He called Luke when he needed a sounding board.

*Damn it, don't start psychoanalyzing your relationships.*

Using the knife, he pulled the flaps back.

A head stared up at him. Black holes sat where the eyes should have been. The face, or what was left of it, was unmistakable. Christian knew it well. He had dreamed of it for months after Bradley Brown's death. This was Brown's mother, decapitated.

A large cross had been carved on her flesh. Deep. The skin rose off the skull in jagged tears, revealing white bone beneath. The slash traveled from the top of her forehead through her nose and lips, leaving her mouth open in a gruesome smile that wanted to stretch for miles.

The horizontal piece of the cross ran across where her eyes should have been. Cuts on either side and dark sockets separating the line.

Christian stared at it for a second, then fell back and landed on his ass.

He pulled his cell phone out and called Tommy.

---

"Hello?" Tommy answered the phone.

"Ineedyoutocometomyhousenow!"

"What? Christian, calm down."

"*Get over here, Tommy!*"

Tommy heard a click. "Hello? Christian, are you there?"

"Is everything okay?" Alice asked from the kitchen.

Tommy put the phone on his lap and stared at it, ignoring the television in front of him. "I don't know. I think I have to go to Christian's house."

"Why? What did he say?" Alice stepped into the living room.

Tommy had been sitting there watching television and smelling the chili cooking, growing hungrier by the second. He had finally grown a pair and asked Alice to move in late last year, bringing her into what had once been only his domain. Even going so far as to introduce her to his two genius-but-weird partners.

"He screamed that I had to get over there."

Alice chuckled. "Well, you better go. Should I set the table for three?"

"I guess." Tommy sighed and stood from the couch. He loved the kid, no doubt about it. His idiosyncrasies and inability to hold his tongue included. Yet, it was still taxing, being Christian's adopted father-figure/friend.

He grabbed his keys and left the house.

It took him ten minutes to drive over. He found Christian standing in the yard, facing the house.

His hands were shaking, and what Tommy could see of his face was as white as an English Bulldog's.

Tommy slammed on the brakes and hopped out of the car.

"Christian, what's wrong?" He trotted from the driveway to where Christian was standing. He was still looking at the box, not even glancing up at the sound of Tommy's voice.

"There's a box. It's on the doorstep." His voice was calm, although his hands shook like he had Parkinson's.

Tommy looked behind him and saw the box. The flaps were open but he couldn't see into it from this distance.

"You want me to go look at it?"

Christian nodded.

Tommy walked across the lawn and squatted next to the box. Using his keys, he carefully lifted the corner of a flap and pulled it back.

"Jesus Christ," he whispered. He squinted at the head, the empty eye sockets giving away who it belonged to. He looked back over his shoulder at Christian, still standing and staring at the road.

Tommy stood up, letting the flap hide the grotesquery again. He reached into his pocket and pulled out his phone.

"Nine-one-one dispatch. What's your emergency?"

"This is FBI Special Agent Thomas Phillips. I need police sent to 3164 Oaklawn Rd."

He answered a few more questions and then ended the call before putting the phone back in his pocket. He went across the lawn and stood next to Christian.

"What are you thinking?"

"Why would someone do that?" Christian asked.

"Do you have an answer?"

"No."

---

Tommy and Christian stood next to Luke in the FBI's autopsy room. Luke stared at the decapitated head.

Roger Linson, the pathologist stood beside the head, holding the tools of his trade.

"Anyone told Waverly yet?" Luke asked. He wouldn't call the FBI Director, but one of his partners might have felt it necessary.

"No," Tommy said.

Christian wasn't looking at the head, or even the table it was sitting on. He leaned against Roger's office window, his hands on the glass and facing the office's interior.

"Do you think he'll want to know?" Luke asked.

"About this? Yeah, because it has to do with Brown, and one of his agents."

Luke nodded and watched as Roger pulled a piece of ravaged skin back a bit farther from the bone. "They did this while she was still alive."

"How do you know?" Christian asked from across the room.

"The raggedness in the cuts. The person wasn't sedated, but twisting and turning while the perpetrator sliced her open."

Luke heard Christian sigh.

"The cross?" Tommy asked. "Do you think that's inspired by Christianity or just a torture method?"

"If it's a torture method, it's an awfully difficult one," Linson said. "The way they cut across the eyes... It's just not necessary to torture someone. They could have done a circle around the outside of her face much easier, without having to deal with the starting and stopping because of the eyeholes. Hell, they could have peeled her face off a lot easier than this."

"Why would they leave it at your door?" Luke asked, wanting to hear the boy's response.

"I don't know," Christian said, surprising Luke. If Luke had his own thoughts, then surely Christian had some as well. Was he not already forming those intuitive videos about what this meant?

"You've got nothing?" Tommy asked, looking over his shoulder at their partner.

"No."

"I checked with the home she was living in," Tommy said. "She went missing two days ago. They alerted the police immediately, but it doesn't appear much was done. They put out a silver alert, but given that Brown's mother couldn't drive they thought they'd find her wandering around somewhere close by."

"How far away is my house from the home?"

"A two-hour drive," Luke added.

Christian straightened up from the window he was leaning against and walked out of the room.

"He's taking it hard," Tommy said.

"Does he think it's his fault she died?" Roger asked.

"I'm not sure. He hasn't really said anything since I got to his house. He shouldn't give a shit. The woman was awful. Just because her son pulled her eyes out of her head, it doesn't grant her penance for what *she* did or what she allowed to happen."

Tommy was right. The woman was a horrible mother and person. Luke didn't care at all about that. "Is the fact that she's Brown's mother important?"

"I don't see how it couldn't be," Tommy answered.

"Then why wouldn't they have dropped the head at my place? I'm the one who killed her son."

Tommy only shook his head.

"You think this is a one and done?" Luke said.

"For Christian's sake, I sure hope so."

———

"Mom, I want to put some police protection around you."

"Nope."

Christian stared at his refrigerator, the phone held to his ear.

"Mom, listen to me. It's important. I think someone might be targeting me."

"Well, maybe you need police around you, then. I don't think anyone is targeting me," she said.

Christian closed his eyes and took in a deep breath.

"I don't know what this person wants, but they're dangerous. I told you what I found. Isn't that enough to make you think you might need some protection?"

"No. You gave me protection two years ago and no one even came looking for me. All they did was crowd our neighborhood and make me drive recklessly because I kept looking in my rearview mirror every five minutes."

"Mom! Don't look in the rearview! You know they're there."

"Can't help it," his mother said. "But no. I'm not going through that again. If someone comes for me, I guess I'll have to deal with it. I'm going to keep living my life as I have."

Christian said nothing. He never felt anger at his mother, and he probably wouldn't classify this emotion as directed *at* her, but her stubbornness instead.

"You're acting like me," he said.

"Who do you think you got it from?"

"I've got to go," Christian said, his hand squeezing his cellphone so hard his knuckles were white.

"Call me when your temper tantrum is done. I love you."

The call went dead and Christian dropped the phone onto his kitchen counter. He had thought the call would go this way. He remembered how much she had hated having the police follow her around while they were hunting for Bradley Brown.

This was different, though. Brown had killed a former

FBI agent, and Waverly had gotten nervous that he might target others with relationships to Tommy, Luke, or Christian. Now, a decapitated head had been laid at Christian's doorstep.

He spent the rest of the day at home, thinking. After being downstairs in Roger's lair, Christian had simply left the office without telling anyone or even taking his computer.

It made no sense. Why would someone kill the old woman, and why would they drop her head off at his house?

His name and address weren't publicly published, but it didn't mean that people couldn't find out where he lived if they wanted. Online tracking was incredible at this point. Virtually no one could live completely off the grid.

Which meant his mother was in danger, too. He wasn't going to let that happen. Losing her wasn't an option.

Christian picked up his cell phone and called Tommy.

"Hey, you doing okay?"

"I'm fine. Listen, can we put some of our people on my mother? I don't want her to see them."

"You've been here two years. How do you not know the answer to this?"

"I don't feel like bullshitting with you," Christian said. "Can we?"

"Yes, under these circumstances, of course," Tommy answered.

"Will you set it up?"

"Sure," Tommy said.

"Thanks." Christian hung up the phone. He didn't know why he felt so angry, but he couldn't stop himself. Tommy had done nothing to him, yet Christian nearly hung up on him, *after* he agreed to help Christian's mother.

He sighed again but didn't place the phone down. He wanted to speak with Luke. Maybe he could connect the pieces Christian couldn't. He found Luke's number.

"You didn't answer any of our calls."

"I know," Christian said. "I'm just... I'm not myself."

"Understandable, given what you found."

"You mind if I come over?"

"No, not at all," Luke said. "When will you be here?"

"Thirty minutes or so."

"See you then."

The line clicked off and Christian let guilt find him again. He had good friends, both Tommy and Luke. He could call them at any time and they'd answer. They would do whatever they could to help him, and yet...

"You've got to get control of yourself," Christian said aloud.

Luke watched the familiar lights flash across his living room. He and Christian had done this many times. The boy came over whenever he needed an intellectual presence in his life. Luke didn't mind his visits. In fact, they helped Luke considerably as well. They allowed him to understand Christian better.

Luke was certain these visits would prove valuable later.

He buzzed the car in and Christian got out of the back. The car pulled off and Luke watched as the young man approached the front door. Brown, shaggy hair, his body thin. He wore a pair of sweatpants and a t-shirt, which he always felt most comfortable in. He was wearing flip-flops, though Luke knew he hated having even those on. Christian hated shoes on general principle, feeling his feet were evolutionarily adapted to deal with the problems of Earth.

Luke opened the door after the first knock. "You're lucky I don't need a lot of sleep."

"You're lucky I do, or else I'd probably be over here a lot more."

"Did you drop in on Tommy?" Luke asked.

"No. I don't think Alice likes it much when I do. Not this late. Maybe not ever, actually."

"Can't blame her," Luke said, smiling.

Christian didn't wait on him to lead the way, but walked from the foyer to the living room, pacing in front of the fireplace as he always did whenever something bothered him.

"Should I tell you to sit down or just let you continue wearing out my floors?"

"Put carpet in, then you won't hear me," Christian said without looking up from his march.

Luke shook his head and sat on the couch. "You want to talk about what you found, or are you having woman problems?"

"None of this is funny, Luke."

"It depends on how you look at it."

"That supposed to be a pun?"

Luke nodded.

"Not a good one." Christian was silent for a second as he reached the opposite wall and turned around. "I can't figure out why someone would give it to *me*. *You* killed Brown. Why wouldn't they send it to you?"

"It depends on what they want to achieve with the head's delivery. Tommy would probably say the why doesn't matter too much, but I think we'd both disagree. It depends on whether they're angry or not."

"What do you mean?"

"Are they angry that Bradley Brown is dead?"

"If they are, then it would have been sent to you," Christian said.

"Possibly."

"What else could it mean?"

"You don't know?"

Christian shook his head, still not looking up. "I don't understand any of this. I can't even make up my mind if the cross had something to do with God, or if it was simply a way to torture the woman."

"Well, one angle is rage. They're mad someone killed Bradley Brown. Like you said, it wouldn't make sense that the head ended up at your house, though. The other, as far as I can see is devotion."

Christian stopped walking. "Devotion?"

"Yes. To you."

"One, why would anybody feel devotion to me? Two, why would they show it like that?"

"Have you lost your ability to think, Christian?" Luke asked. "These are simple questions."

"Enlighten me, then."

"Well, as far as your first question, they'd have to be crazy to feel devotion to you, but that's the business we're in." Luke smiled and continued, "Why they feel such devotion could be down to any number of reasons, but if it's true, then killing Bradley Brown's mother makes a lot of sense. She gave birth to the person who tried to kill you."

"Leaders who inspire that kind of devotion have cults or authoritarian dictatorships. I live by myself and haven't ever been on a date. It doesn't add up."

*No, it doesn't,* Luke thought. *All your brains and you still don't understand the simplicity of chaos. It's beyond your grasp because of your need for order and purpose.*

"Christian, when have you heard of a decapitated head adding up to something that makes sense? It might be time to expand your horizons."

"Okay. Say you're right. Let's play it out. No one else has tried to kill me, so how else would he show his devotion?"

"If we figure that out," Luke said, "we won't have to worry about anyone else dying."

# CHAPTER FIVE

"Today the FBI discovered the decapitated head of Mrs. Lorraine Brown, the mother of deceased serial killer Bradley Brown. She was abducted from the state-run assisted living facility she resided in before being brutally murdered. When inquiries were made, the FBI responded that they are investigating this crime as they would any other. No further information was given at this time."

Lucy stood and walked to the television, turning it off.

She remained in front of the black box for a bit, a smile bright over her thin face. Her right eye twitched at the corner, though she didn't realize it. Lucy had better control over herself now, but when she really got to thinking about something, she forgot to control the tics and stuttering.

Christian had seen what she left for him.

Lucy knew he didn't understand what it meant yet, but that was okay. The point of the woman's head was to show him that *it* was beginning. Nothing else.

Lucy wasn't sure when they'd find the rest of Mrs. Brown's remains, but she wasn't concerned. She had done her deeds in an old warehouse. She shoved a sock so far down the woman's throat, that she'd been worried it might suffocate her. Lucy needed the woman alive the entire time if God's plan was to be followed.

Sacrifice was what mattered here. Sacrifice and suffering.

At first, Lucy had questioned that mentality, as the Old Testament said sacrifice was only given to God. Of course, she realized the error of her thoughts after a bit more thinking. She *was* giving sacrifice to God, through Christian Windsor.

Next week, the halfway house would give Lucy even greater privileges. She would be free to come and go as she pleased. She'd be subject to random drug tests and the like, but that was fine. Lucy had never been a drug user and certainly didn't plan on starting. Not with what God had placed in front of her.

He hadn't shown her who came next.

One sacrifice was only the beginning.

Christian Windsor needed many, *many* more before he would finally understand what he was supposed to do.

*Please show me the way, Lord,* Lucy prayed.

---

Ryan Goleen was twenty-nine years old. He worked at a local auto parts store just north of Atlanta, Georgia. He absolutely never thought about Christian Windsor anymore. He'd heard his name mentioned a few years back when that serial killer was caught and had felt a momentary sense of guilt at the name. Other than that, though,

Christian Windsor was from a past that Ryan preferred not to think about.

He'd been an asshole when he was younger, for lack of a better term.

Except, even that wasn't truthful. By the age of sixteen, Ryan had been a bona fide alcoholic, if undiagnosed. He drank every weekend with his friends, not to mention making sure he had a few shots before school, and any pills he could get his hands on as well.

Christian Windsor had changed the direction of Ryan's life, even if Christian never knew it. Ryan certainly didn't, not at the time. He had thought that when he caught Christian again, he'd put the bastard in a coma for all the trouble he'd ended up in.

At the time, Ryan considered what they'd done no more than a prank. Now Ryan realized how cruel he'd been, but the twelve steps taught that you couldn't dwell in the past, and so Ryan did his best not to.

The district attorney could have charged Ryan with attempted murder, but luckily, he had dropped it down to reckless endangerment. Ryan had done six months in juvenile, and when he came out, he'd apologized to Christian for what happened. Apologized and meant it. Christian, for his part, had been as weird as always and said nothing.

The twelve steps said you couldn't control what other people did, only yourself. An apology was all he could give.

From sixteen until twenty-nine, Ryan didn't take another sip of alcohol besides once, when he ordered a nonalcoholic beer, which the waitress got wrong—but he didn't count it against his sobriety. At twenty-nine, his juvenile record was expunged and he had no rap sheet. He managed the auto parts store, went home to his wife and two-year-old son every night, and the three went to church every Sunday.

He never thought about Christian Windsor, and certainly never thought about the single news article that had been written about him twelve years ago.

---

God was good.

Lucy had known that from her earliest days, but He had been especially good this evening.

Lucy sat at a computer reading the old news article. She had been confused about who to sacrifice next. The first person had been obvious from the moment the Lord put Christian Windsor in front of her. But for the past week, she'd struggled with God's silence. Even when she stared at pictures of Christian on the computer, the Lord didn't speak.

She had to keep faith. That's what He was teaching her. Keep faith that no matter what happened, as long as she trusted in Him, then He'd lead her correctly.

Lucy had been searching each night for hints about Christian Windsor's past, hoping to find anyone that might have wronged him. She understood how smart he was. A gift from God if there ever had been one. Articles abounded about Christian's accomplishments in school, not to mention what he managed to do about that awful Bradley Brown. A lot of the credit went to his partner, Luke Titan, who Lucy felt had received far too much adulation for Brown's death, but there were quite a few profiles on Christian as well.

Finally, Lucy decided to go farther back in his life. To try and understand if something might have happened when he was younger.

Bingo.

*God was good.*

She stared at the article, reading the name again and again. Ryan Goleen. *He* had tried to harm Christian Windsor, God's chosen one. Lucy was getting good at navigating the Internet. She spent five dollars for Goleen's address from a website called Spokeo. She entered that address into an online mapping service and saw that he lived three hours north of her.

Lucy's jaw tightened, causing her mouth to shift into an ugly, strained frown. No one was around to see, but if anyone had asked, she would have said she was smiling.

Lucy was happy, after all.

---

*The Gwinnett County Tribune*
*September 24th*
*Issue 504*
*Local News*

*Football Game Shut Down After Near Death*

*Ryan Goleen was arrested on Friday night at the Grayson High School football game. Each season, there are a few incidents of students arrested for underage drinking—a misdemeanor by state laws. The single arrest that occurred on Friday night had nothing to do with alcohol.*

*Fellow student, Christian Windsor is in critical condition at the hospital, due to what police say was a "cold and poorly thought out prank." The Police Chief further stated, "High school pranks are one thing, and bullying is another. This goes way beyond both of those."*

*Christian Windsor was found by Grayson High School's head coach during halftime of the football game. The team was convening in the field house, where they spend the off-season training. Coach Mike Cahn found the fifteen-year-old lying on one of the weight benches, a barbell weighted down with two hundred and fifty pounds across his chest.*

*"I don't want to talk about what the kid looked like," Coach Cahn told the paper. "I just hope that whoever did this, if it was Goleen, or someone else, they get the correct punishment for it."*

*Allegedly, Ryan Goleen and a number of unnamed accomplices forced Christian Windsor onto the bench before lowering the barbell onto his chest. A very heavy weight, it was impossible for the junior class student to lift it off by himself. Eventually, he passed out.*

*Windsor's family has not released a statement, and Ryan Goleen is being held in the county jail. Judge Lewis Kinnip has not yet issued a ruling on the possibility of bail.*

# CHAPTER SIX

Ryan opened his eyes and found himself in what appeared to be a storage unit. In front of him was a large, metal, hanging door. It was closed. Ryan couldn't tell if it was locked but...

*But what? What am I doing in here?*

Panic grabbed him with rough hands. He looked down and saw he sat naked on a wooden chair, his arms and legs bound by metal wires.

*"Hello!"* he shouted.

His voice echoed off the walls around him. When it died, he sat in silence again.

*"Hellooooo!"* he screamed, louder this time. He kept going, switching between *"Help!"* and *"Hello!"* but no response came, and after ten minutes or so, he fell quiet.

Ryan closed his eyes tightly.

*Did I get drunk? Is that why I can't remember?*

It had been years since his last sip, but that fear always rested in the back of his mind that he might slip up and everything he'd worked so hard for would drown in a pint of vodka.

But no, he didn't feel hungover.

*Then how the hell did I end up in here?*

He opened his eyes and searched the storage unit, looking for anything; clothes, a cellphone, something that might give him a clue.

He saw nothing but cold concrete and metal walls. He and Kerry owned a storage unit, but how often did they go to it? Rarely. Most people might visit a storage unit once a year at most, which meant no one would be around to hear him now. Sure, someone probably sat in the front office, but clearly, his voice wasn't reaching them.

Ryan jerked against the wires, but that only drove them deeper into his flesh, getting him no closer to freedom.

He sighed and closed his eyes.

*Let go and let God.*

Ryan started praying, the same thing he'd done the past decade and a half whenever he needed help.

---

Lucy was nervous about leaving Ryan Goleen in the storage unit overnight. She knew she shouldn't be, that such doubt was incompatible with the faith God deserved. Still, if something went wrong, if he somehow alerted someone, or the owner got nosey and started poking around in different units, Lucy was done.

That wouldn't happen, though. If God was for her, who could be against her?

Lucy had decided after cutting off Brown's head, that

she wanted to do something in closer quarters. She might want to keep people for a time, and having them in an open warehouse—even if deserted—created risk. So she found a storage company south of Atlanta.

It was pretty much in the middle of nowhere, and the owner was an eighty-year-old man who was hard of hearing. She had been to quite a few storage units, but this one seemed best suited for her purpose. Out of the way, a large area, and with an owner who didn't seem very mobile.

Lucy had gotten off work an hour ago and had her scheduled appointment with Dr. Brigham. One of the conditions of her release was to continue therapy. She didn't mind it. These conversations just gave her more opportunities to show the world how she had *changed*, and how well the system worked for her.

Lucy understood from her father that people wanted self-congratulation when they should only want to glorify God. By doing this, Lucy was feeding right into what Dr. Brigham and the whole establishment needed.

*Look at what we've done, all ye. Look at how great we are, how we've helped this poor, pathetic girl. She is cured.*

A bunch of sinners, not to mention idiots.

"Hey, Lucy, how are you doing?"

Lucy looked up from the Bible on her lap. Dr. Brigham stood next to the chair, having snuck up on her. She didn't like that one bit. She hated being surprised. He should have announced himself.

"I'm good," she said, her left eyebrow twitching slightly, the only sign that showed her displeasure. She cleared her throat. "How are yuh-you?"

"I'm well," the doctor said. "Would you like to get started?"

Lucy nodded and placed her bookmark in her Bible. She stood and the two of them walked through the halfway house's common area to the meeting rooms in the back. Dr. Brigham checked the schedule on the wall before leading them to their assigned room.

"How has the last week been?" Dr. Brigham asked once they were both seated.

"Good."

"You'll have to do better than that, Lucy. I know that you don't speak a lot because you're scared of stuttering. You don't have to be scared of that, okay?"

Lucy nodded. She didn't believe a word the man said, knowing that if she started stuttering again they'd throw her right back in Greenbriar Lakes. Not to mention, Daddy had taught her all she needed to know about her stuttering.

*What would happen to Ryan Goleen, then? He'd starve to death, the poor man.*

Lucy smiled at the thought.

"Is something funny?" the doctor asked, his own slight grin appearing.

"No," Lucy said, smiling wider at the thought of Goleen's skeleton sitting in the chair, most of his flesh having been devoured by rats and ants.

Dr. Brigham chuckled. "Well, it must be *something*."

"Just a joke someone said in here."

Dr. Brigham remained smiling and after a few seconds said, "How is your job?"

"Good. It's e-easy."

"I thought it would be. You're a smart woman, Lucy."

"Thu-thank you."

"I'd like to start discussing what you want to do when you leave here. Another few months and they're going to help you get your own place," Dr. Brigham said. "Have you given any thought to it?"

Lucy nodded. She'd thought of nothing else since she arrived, though they weren't *her* plans, but God's. "I'd like to join a church."

*Don't smile. Don't smile*, she thought repeatedly. Yes, she'd join a church. Or rather, she'd create one.

"I think that's a great idea! You know you don't have to wait until you get out of here to do that."

Lucy nodded but said nothing.

"Come on, Lucy. Talk to me. Why don't you want to join one now?'

"Be-because I might not live in this area. I wuh-wouldn't be able to travel v-very far."

"Ah, that makes sense," Dr. Brigham said. "Smart. How are things going here? Do you like it?"

She nodded again.

"Have you made any friends?"

"No."

"I think it's important that you do, Lucy. You're going to need a support system when you leave here to make sure you don't let your anger get the best of you again. Having friends, people you can talk to, can all help you mitigate your thoughts when they become overwhelming. Have you at least talked to people here?"

Lucy nodded again. She had barely said four words even during group therapy.

"With who?"

Lucy smiled and looked down at the table in front of her. She didn't want to smile but did it because this was an *essential* conversation, and the smile would allow her lie to go without punishment. A stupid lie. A stupid, stupid lie. At least if she was going to do it, she should have had a story ready.

"It's okay," Dr. Brigham said. "You don't have to be best friends with everyone, but I would like you to start trying, okay?"

Lucy nodded, looking up at the doctor with the most trusting face she could muster. She'd start talking, just as soon as she woke up tomorrow.

———

The cab dropped Lucy off two blocks from the storage unit she'd rented. Her rent at the halfway house was nearly nothing, and she was making more money than she ever had before and saving most of it since she didn't go anywhere.

She walked the two blocks and pulled out the key to the unit. She knelt and stuck it in the padlock. Before she turned it, she looked around, her eyes narrowed like a rat wanting to venture from its lair for a morsel of food, but knowing predators might be around.

Lucy scanned the area. She saw only the sun reflecting off the metal units. She removed the padlock and lifted the door open about two feet before bending over and slipping underneath it.

She closed it behind her.

Goleen was sitting where she'd left him. Getting him

there had been a chore, no doubt about it. She'd snagged him when he was getting off work, having watched him carefully each evening for a few nights. He always parked in the back and always left at the same time.

Had Lucy been someone else, she would have realized the risk was far too large and abandoned the plan altogether. However, Lucy knew God wasn't going to let any heathens get in the way of His plans. She'd simply stepped away from the dumpster she'd been hiding behind and clocked Ryan Goleen with a rock. He'd collapsed and she'd dragged him to her car and thrown him in the trunk.

For someone her size, Lucy was incredibly strong.

"Who are you?" Goleen asked.

He was sweating profusely, which was something Lucy *hadn't* thought about. The temperature outside was in the eighties, and already she felt her own brow growing wet. If she didn't get the man some water, he'd die before she could do what was needed.

"I'm Lucy," she said.

"What are you doing, Lucy?" Goleen said. His voice was strained, but obviously trying to remain calm.

Lucy walked by him and went to the bag that sat against the back wall. It was a baseball bat bag that she'd bought for seven dollars at a used sports store before she went to work on Mrs. Brown. She slung it over her shoulder and walked back in front of Goleen.

"I'm preparing you for the person you're going to meet." No stutter, not even the thought of one.

"Lucy, please. Listen to me. I have a kid and a wife. Whatever..." The man let out a short sob, nearing the edge of a breakdown, but regained control of himself. "Whatever you're going to do. Let's just talk about it first, okay?"

"Sure," Lucy said. She placed the bat bag down and pulled out the tripod. *That* had put her back two hundred dollars, but it was worth it. The Lord needed a way to speak to the world, after all. Money didn't matter to Lucy. Did the bird stress about where its next meal would come from? No. Didn't God love His children more than the birds? So why would Lucy worry?

"What… What are you going to do with that?"

Lucy was setting up the camera about ten feet from Goleen. "I'm going to record you."

"Why?"

"Because it's essential."

"But *why?*" the man said, his voice straining louder.

"The Lord once looked for a single good person in Sodom and Gomorrah. He said if one good man could be found, then he'd save the cities. The only thing was, they couldn't find one. God was forced to destroy the city and anyone in it. He even turned Lot's wife into a pillar of salt—"

*"Because she looked back!"* the man shouted. *"Because she disobeyed God's order!"*

Lucy smiled and looked out from behind the camera for a second. "That's right. Some people, fake Christians as I call them, believe all those stories from the Old Testament are just that, *stories*. They believe they're just meant to show a *meaning*. Not me. Every word of the Bible is true as far as I'm concerned."

She was quiet for a second and looked through the camera lens. She had no awareness of her stutter's disappearance. "God has commanded me to do something, and that's the only *why* that matters. It's not that I'm afraid He'll turn me into a pillar of salt, though He could if He wanted. It's that when God says to do something, you do it."

"Look, please. Please. Just listen to me. I believe in God. I pray every day. I love Him with all my heart. He doesn't want you to do this. What about thou *shalt* not kill?"

Lucy looked down at her feet, still smiling. "I wonder if lambs could speak, would they say the same at their sacrifice?" She looked at Goleen. "I think they would have."

Lucy went to her bag and pulled out a ski mask, setting it to the side for a moment. She then pulled out a long, black shirt and a pair of men's sweatpants. She put them both on, her arms moving in jerky spasms as she dressed. Lucy didn't see Goleen's head cock to the side, surprised—even given everything happening—at the way she moved.

Finally, she put the ski mask over her face.

"All right. Let's get started."

# CHAPTER SEVEN

Stuttering had been the first noticeable problem Lucy faced as a child, though it stemmed from something else. She'd never considered what that might be, and neither did anyone else in her life.

The stuttering started when she was around eight years old.

She didn't remember the first time she couldn't get a word out correctly, but she *did* remember the first time Daddy caught wind of it.

He, Mommy, and Lucy had all been sitting at the kitchen table. Lucy even remembered the food that had been on the table before them: mashed potatoes, green beans, and meat loaf.

"C-c-can you puh-puh-pass the mashed puh-puh-puh-potatoes?"

She hadn't noticed how different her words sounded. She was only concerned with getting her food. When her father didn't move, she looked up from the bowl she'd been asking for. Daddy was staring at her.

"What did you say?"

"Cuh-cuh-can—"

"*Stop!*" her father shouted and slammed his fist down on the table. The silverware bounced in front of Lucy. She felt her bladder suddenly grow full. "Say it again."

Tears welled in Lucy's eyes, making her parents appear hazy. She knew not to dawdle, though. "C-c-c-c-c—" but she couldn't get the word out. She stopped, pausing briefly, and then tried again. "C-c-c-c-c."

The only noise that came from her mouth was the sound *cuh.*

"Shut up," Daddy said. "Shut your mouth." He looked at Mommy. "This is your fault, you know that? All the babying made it so she cain't even talk now." He turned his glare back on Lucy. "You're not getting a single piece of food until you can say it right."

The tears spilled from Lucy's eyes. They rolled down her pale cheeks like huge rain drops down glass. She didn't want to try speaking again because she knew what the result would be. Lucy wasn't going to be able to say anything without stuttering, especially not now.

"Say it again."

"D-d-d-daddy, puh-puh-puh-please." She could barely talk at all. She was almost unable to get anything out.

"*Shut up! Stop that damned stutterin'!*"

Lucy had sat there without saying another word. Her father didn't break eye contact, not when he put more food onto his plate, nor when he chewed. No one said anything for the rest of dinner, and Lucy's plate remained empty. She knew better than to get up and leave. Daddy might need to tell her to quit stuttering, but not that it was a *very* bad idea to leave without his permission.

Finally, when her father had finished his third plate, he'd stood and walked out of the kitchen.

Lucy's mother dutifully started cleaning up without glancing at her daughter. It took Lucy a moment, but she began picking up the silverware and food as well, just as she did every night.

Lucy didn't want to upset Daddy any further.

# CHAPTER EIGHT

Tommy rarely received calls from Director Alan Waverly. Tommy, Luke, and Christian had all met with him during Bradley Brown's spree, but since then, Tommy might have seen one or two emails from the man.

Now, the three of them were in Tommy's office, and Waverly's voice filled it through the speakerphone.

"How bad is it?"

"It's bad, sir," Tommy said.

"With what was in the paper this morning, do you believe this is religious? They're calling the killer the Priest."

"Yes, we think this is religion-based," Luke said. "There's really not any other way to view what happened."

"Okay, just so I'm straight on what exactly happened before I have this damned press conference in three hours. The victim is Ryan Goleen. Four hours ago, a video arrived at three national newspapers, as well as on Christian's doorstep. The video shows a ritualistic killing. Right now, we have no other leads, though obviously, we think this is connected to the murder of Bradley Brown's mother. Am I missing anything?"

"Sir," Christian tried to reply, but only a whisper came out. He cleared his throat and spoke again. "Sir, there's more. I, um, I went to high school with Ryan Goleen."

Tommy's mouth dropped open. His eyes flashed to Christian and he caught a small smile appearing on Luke's face. They'd been working on this all morning. They had no body, but the Priest, as the press was calling the murderer, had been happy to show the camera the dead man's ID.

The whole time, Christian hadn't said a word about knowing the man.

*Has he said much in the past four hours?*

Christian stared at Tommy's desk.

Five seconds passed and then Waverly said, "What was that?"

"I went to high school with him." Christian didn't blink. Didn't move in the slightest.

*He's in shock,* Tommy thought.

"Jesus Christ, Windsor. Were you going to tell us this?"

"I, um. I'm sorry. I…"

"Sir," Tommy interjected, "can you give us one second, please?" He didn't wait for an answer but hit mute on the speakerphone. "Hey, Christian. Look at me." The kid's face slowly turned to his. "What you say over the next few minutes is extremely important for your career. We can worry about all the rest later, but right now, you need to turn that mind of yours on, okay?"

Christian looked dazed.

"Do you hear me, Christian?"

The kid blinked and Tommy saw him snap out of his fugue.

"There. Tell Waverly what you know and I'll get him off the phone. Don't worry about anything besides this one conversation, you got it?"

Christian nodded.

"Sorry about that, sir," Tommy said. "We're here."

Christian wasted no time. "I'm extremely sorry, sir. I wasn't one hundred percent certain it was the same person until right before this call. I should have looked it up sooner and I apologize. To be honest, I didn't even recognize the name at first."

Another pause from the Director's side. "I need to know what you know about him."

"Yes, sir. I'll have it in a report to you within the next hour."

Waverly sighed, but his voice didn't soften. "Within the hour, and then the three of us talk in two more. Everyone understand?"

"Yes, sir," Tommy said, the other two echoing him.

The speakerphone clicked and the line was cut.

"Jesus," Tommy said, leaning back in his chair.

Luke adjusted his own, turning it so that he faced Christian. "An interesting turn of events."

"I don't know why I didn't say anything. Everything I just told Waverly was bullshit. I knew it was him from the moment I saw the video. The guy... I didn't have much trouble in high school with people. I did their homework, let them copy from me, and that pretty much protected me from bullies. Except for Goleen. He put me in a coma."

Christian wasn't looking at either of them. He had gone back to staring at the desk.

"He went to juvie for a little while. The guy's family life was horrible, but I think he found religion in juvie. When he got out he made it a point to apologize to me. I just stared at him. We never spoke again."

"This changes things, Christian," Tommy said. "It means whoever is doing this is doing it to people that have harmed you, or tried to harm you. We've got an hour to get a report to Waverly. We need every single name of anyone who has ever bullied you, or could be considered an enemy."

---

The night had grown late and the room was dark except for the television screen. Luke made sure to get a copy of the video before he left, downloading it onto a thumb drive. The three didn't leave the office until nearly two, even Christian pushing through his exhaustion to get everything Waverly asked for.

Luke was alone now and he wanted to see the video again, because it was, in its own way, glorious.

He hit play on his remote and the stereo system took control, pushing the silence away.

They called the murderer a "priest," but as Luke watched him move across the screen, he wondered if the papers were correct about that. The perpetrator took great lengths to make their body look androgynous, but Luke thought the frame beneath the baggy clothes was that of a woman. A thin one, who clearly had abnormalities with her nervous system. Perhaps the Priest*ess* was a better moniker.

The killer's gender didn't really matter at the moment, however.

The Priest had obviously put a lot of work into planning this, wanting to truly create a show.

Luke watched as Goleen was stretched upward, first by his left hand and then by his right. The Priest had attached rings at the top of the metal room and then tossed a thick rope through each one. Apparently, he or she was strong enough to hoist a fully grown man up by pulling the rope through one ring, tying it off, and then moving to the other side.

When the killer was done, Ryan Goleen hung suspended ten feet in the air.

Not quite a cross, but close.

The Priest disappeared from the camera frame for a few moments, then came in from the side carrying a baseball bat. She swung it at his right knee. Goleen's breaking bones echoed in the small metal chamber. The noise was drowned out by the man's screaming, however.

The Priest wasted no time. The screams didn't matter in the slightest to him or her. The bat came down on the second kneecap.

Unnecessary, but symbolic.

Christ had died for the sins of men, but not a bone on his body had been broken. This man clearly wasn't meant to represent Christ, but a sinner like those who hung beside Christ. He had endured the same punishment as all Roman criminals.

"This man broke one of *your* laws, didn't he?" Luke said.

The man continued screaming and Luke hit fast forward, cutting off the horrific noise. He turned the speed up to five times, as the video covered multiple days. The Priest came back sometimes, using a ladder to give the man water before leaving.

Ryan Goleen simply hung in the air until he suffocated, his lungs collapsing inside his chest. An *extremely* painful way to go, like drowning except over a much longer time period. Poor Mr. Goleen also had to deal with his shoulder ligaments slowly ripping apart.

"I wonder," Luke said. "Is Christian your God, or is your God pointing you toward Christian? Is there even a difference?"

---

Christian sat in his mother's living room. He couldn't imagine going to his house. He had moved out of his mother's at twenty-three, and only because she somewhat forced him. It wasn't that she said he couldn't stay, but she knew when it was time for him to leave, and in her own way, she nudged him out.

She simply raised his rent until it was cheaper to live somewhere else.

Tonight, though, he found himself needing to be near her.

"Do you want some milk, honey?" she called from the kitchen.

The moment he'd told her he was going to spend the night, she had started busying herself with dinner and dessert. It didn't matter if he was staying one night or two weeks, he would have more food than he could eat.

"No."

Christian stared at the television, which was showing an older program he didn't recognize. He'd never had much use for television, but his mother enjoyed it. After what happened today, it didn't matter what was playing.

"Dinner should be ready in a half hour," his mother said as she walked into the living room.

She was approaching her sixties, although she looked a decade younger. Christian thought it was because she *never* worried, which meant he'd probably look ten years *older* when he was her age.

"What's bothering you?" she asked, taking a seat next to him and putting her hand on his leg.

No one else moved like that around him, and he wouldn't have known how to react if they had. With his mom, though, it all felt natural.

"You're still not watching the news?" he asked.

"Nope. Not since that Bradley Brown nonsense. It scares me too much thinking about the people you're trying to catch. If it's something I need to know, I figure Carla down the street will let me know."

"She didn't come talk to you today?" he asked.

"No. Now tell me, what's going on?"

"You remember when I was put in that coma?"

"No. When did that happen?"

"This is serious, Mom," Christian said. "Don't joke. The kid that did it to me, his name was Ryan Goleen." He shook his head, trying to gather his thoughts. He'd been a step behind the entire day. "Okay, first, Bradley Brown... Look, I don't know any other way to say this..."

"Honey, I'm your mother. Just talk to me," she said.

He nodded. She was right. This wasn't work, and he didn't need to have a preamble or disclaimer.

"Bradley Brown's mother was murdered," Christian said. "Her head was put in a box and left on my doorstep. I didn't tell you what happened, only that people around me might be targeted. Today, a video showed up of Ryan Goleen. He was tortured before they murdered him. The video was delivered to my house, as well as to some pretty big newspapers."

His mother didn't gasp or remove her hand and put it over her mouth. She knew better than to react like that when Christian was in such a state, and he was glad for it. She was bedrock, and he needed that now.

"Has anyone given a reason for it?" she asked after a few seconds.

"No."

"Have you been able to *see* anything about it? About the man killing these people?"

He knew what she meant. Had he gone inside his mansion? He shook his head. "I don't want to." He felt himself about to break, the tears that had been threatening to swell all day finally rising up. "This is my fault. It's different than last time, Mom. These people are dying *because of me*."

"No, no, honey. No, they're not." His mother took his head in her arm and pulled him close. At twenty-five years old, Christian cried while he held his mother, without a single thought of embarrassment. "These people are dying because a crazy person is killing them. If someone put Carla's head on my doorstep, would you say it's my fault?"

"No, but..."

"But nothing. If it wouldn't be my fault, then it's not yours either. I won't hear any more about that."

"Mom, if I wasn't out there in the public eye, this wouldn't be happening. Ryan Goleen would still be alive. I looked him up today. He hasn't been in any trouble since that one incident. He turned his whole life around, and now he's dead."

"Oh, honey, if you didn't exist, then this crazy person would have simply killed someone else, and then it would just be another person dead. They wouldn't have known you at all. This isn't about you. It's about whatever is wrong in that person's head. It's not your fault. It isn't."

The two sat in silence for a few minutes, holding each other. His mother ran her hands through his hair until his tears finally stopped.

"It's your job to catch these people, the ones that are hurting others. Whatever this sicko is thinking, it's your job to make sure he stops."

Christian nodded, but he didn't let go of his mother.

---

The phone woke Christian. It was buzzing on the nightstand next to his bed. He looked at the time as he picked it up, seeing that it was nearing eleven in the morning.

"Hello?" he mumbled, kicking himself for sleeping in this late. It didn't matter that it was Saturday. Neither

Tommy nor Luke would still be in bed, and what his mother said last night was the truth. It was his job to stop this person.

"Hi, Christian? It's Veronica Lopez. How are you?"

Christian blinked as the name came to him. He remembered every time he'd seen or spoken with the woman, but the first memory that surfaced was her lying on Bradley Brown's couch, bound and scared.

"I've had better weeks." He said nothing else, realizing he probably sounded rude, but truly unsure what else to say.

"You've had worse ones, too, I'm sure," Veronica said. "I was wondering if we could meet sometime this week? Not to discuss Luke," she said and laughed.

The last time they'd met privately, both thought Luke was involved in something nefarious, perhaps even murder.

"About what?" Christian asked.

"Well, I'd like to explain it in person, if that's okay? It'll just be easier."

Christian sighed. "Okay, but I'm pretty busy right now with everything that's happening. You'll have to come by the office."

"That's fine. Tuesday morning work?"

"Sure."

"Thanks a lot, Christian. I'll see you then."

He hung the phone up without saying anything and let it drop beside him. He leaned his head back on the pillow and looked up at the ceiling. He knew he would have missed calls from Luke, given their task today. He could smell pancakes cooking down the hall. His mother had clearly expected him to sleep in after their talk last night.

"You're avoiding it," Christian asked himself. "Why?"

He was talking about his mansion. He hadn't gone to it this entire time, although he knew things were starting to form inside. His mind was beginning to formulate ideas about whoever was doing this, yet Christian didn't want to see them.

He was scared, in a way that he hadn't been with the Brown case.

"Not yet," he said.

He got out of bed, and after using the bathroom, walked down the hall to the kitchen.

"Good morning," his mom said.

"Hey."

Christian sat down at the kitchen table, and a plate with three pancakes was placed in front of him, as though he were at a restaurant. "Thank you," he said, reaching for the butter and syrup already on the table.

"You're welcome. Are you feeling any better?"

"Some."

"Do you have plans today?"

Christian nodded as he poured syrup onto his food, the sugar coating everything. "I'm going to talk with Goleen's wife."

---

Christian stood to the left of the door and Luke to the right.

Luke reached up and pressed the doorbell. Christian

stood with his hands in his pockets, consciously knowing how childish he probably looked, but unable to pull them out. He didn't want to be here but knew it was the right thing to do. Tommy could have come instead, but Ryan Goleen wasn't dead because of Tommy.

"Hi, can I help you?" the woman said after opening the front door. She had long brown hair and a thin, pretty face, but her eyes looked haunted.

Christian was sure they were. Haunted by a priest.

Luke showed her his badge. "Hi, Mrs. Goleen. I'm Special Agent Luke Titan, and this is Agent Christian Windsor. Thank you for allowing us to come talk with you today. We'd both like to offer our condolences for your loss."

Christian nodded as Luke spoke.

"Come on in," she said, stepping back. She was wearing a robe despite it being three in the afternoon. "Britt's at her grandparents. I'm picking her up today."

The woman led them through the house, and despite the haunting in her eyes, she kept her voice level as she spoke.

"Would either of you like something to drink? I've got soft drinks, water, some liquor if you'd like."

"No, ma'am. Thank you, but we're on duty. We'd prefer to get out of your way as quickly as possible," Luke said.

The three of them sat down in the living room.

"We have the statement that you gave the police," Luke began, "but we'd like to follow up on a few specific items. If you need to stop at all, please let us know and we can come back another time."

Christian admired Luke's ability to show such

sympathy while remaining calm and to the point. Christian was having a tough time holding himself together as he looked around the man's house. He saw pictures of Goleen's daughter, Brittany hanging on the walls.

"I'll let you know," she said. "What do you want to ask?"

"Had your husband discussed my partner with you, or anyone else, lately? Had anyone that you know of asked him about what happened in high school?"

Mrs. Goleen looked directly at Christian, and he saw a woman who would never heal from what happened to her husband. She'd seen the videos. The wounds were fresh now and would probably heal on the surface, but deep down where they really hurt, they'd never scar over.

"He was thankful for you. You, or what happened after you, changed his life. It took him a long time to forgive himself for what he did, but he eventually did. He said that he apologized to you once?"

Christian nodded. "That's true."

"What did you say to him?"

"I just stared, I think. I'm not very good at communicating."

She nodded, her eyes narrowing. "Yeah, I can see that. I can see why people might have picked on you back then, or wanted to, anyway. Ryan said you were a brainiac?"

"I guess you could say that."

Mrs. Goleen looked back at Luke. "No. No one ever mentioned what happened back then, and he didn't talk about it anymore, either. It was something a long time in the past, and he'd moved on." She paused and looked at their empty hands. "Do either of you need to write any of this down?"

"No," Luke said. "We'll remember."

"You're a brainiac, too, I take it?" she asked.

Luke gave a self-deprecating smile. "I guess you could say that. Mrs. Goleen, we'd like to put some surveillance on your house, if that's okay. We think there is a chance that whoever did this to your husband might come after you."

"Why me? I don't know him," she said as if Christian wasn't there.

"No, but you were married to someone who hurt Christian. We think this person might be obsessed with Agent Windsor, and that puts you and your daughter at risk."

Mrs. Goleen didn't say anything for a moment, then she finally nodded. "Okay."

"Thank you. They'll be here within thirty minutes of us leaving. Most likely, you'll never know they're around. They'll blend in with the surroundings unless they need to make themselves known."

"Okay. What—"

"Mrs. Goleen," Christian interrupted. "Would it be okay with you if I attend the funeral?"

The woman turned her face back to him. Tears were in her eyes. She nodded.

"Thank you," Christian said. "I don't have a lot of questions to ask, and I'm sorry about that. I know this isn't easy, having us here." He looked down at his feet, not fully sure where he was going with this but unable to stop himself from continuing. "I just wanted to say I'm going to find whoever did it. I'm going to find them and I'm going to stop them."

"Thanks, but I wish you would have done that after the head showed up at your door."

———

"Veronica Lopez called me," Christian said. "Are you still her shrink?"

"Yes," Luke said.

"Any idea why she's calling?"

Luke looked at his rearview mirror as he pulled away from the curb. Christian was avoiding what happened inside the house and Mrs. Goleen's ruthless response to Christian's heartfelt—if childish—pledge. Luke had wanted to smile at the woman but kept his lips still.

"I recommended it."

"Why?" Christian asked.

"I think you two might be able to help each other. She's ready to write again, and you need to talk to someone other than your mother, so I thought I'd recommend this."

"Are you trying to set us up romantically?"

"No," Luke said. "But if something happened, you could do much worse."

The car went quiet after that. "Are you blaming yourself?" he asked after a few minutes.

"Yes."

"Do you really think this is your fault, or are you feeling what you think you *should* be feeling?"

"What do you mean?" Christian asked.

Luke knew he understood the question perfectly. He didn't want to answer it, was all. "You know what I mean.

Are you avoiding it because you're afraid to tell me the truth, or because you want to know why I'm asking it?"

Christian looked over from his seat. "Why you're asking it."

"Well, logically, there's no reason for you to feel guilty. You're no guiltier of this than an ant queen is when her worker drones bring back the entrails of a dead beetle."

"There's no guilt in that at all. That's nature. This isn't nature. There's no need to kill humans to survive. That's a horrible analogy, Luke."

"Only if you're seeing this through your own schema. If you looked through the Priest's, you'd see it as a very apt analogy. You're the queen, and this Priest is the worker drone. His survival depends on yours. Actually, his entire world's survival depends on yours, and so he must bring you the beetle. He must keep bringing you more beetles if he wants to ensure that the world continues spinning. Now, answer my question, do you actually feel guilty?"

"Yes," Christian said.

Luke believed him. Christian's guilt was good, something that could be used and stretched for a long, long time. "It's affecting your work."

"I know."

"Do you have any plans to mitigate it?"

"The guilt, or the effects?"

"The effects. I don't think Mrs. Goleen cares too much about your guilt, given our conversation," Luke said.

"Yeah, Luke, I'd like to, but I don't fucking know how."

Luke smiled internally. Rage and guilt were just fine. Luke could deal extensively with those emotions.

# CHAPTER NINE

Lucy dreamed about Ryan Goleen. She couldn't help it.

In her dreams, he swung from his restraints, his arms attached to the ropes on either side of him. Lucy saw the way his muscles and ligaments stretched, and his shoulder eventually popping out of its socket.

She woke with a smile.

Of course, what mattered wasn't her enjoyment, but Christian changing into what the Lord desired, but Lucy found herself having some fun, which she thought was okay, too.

Lucy hadn't been able to stay with Goleen the whole time, although she would have liked to. She had her own copy of the video, but nowhere to watch it yet. Instead, she relied on her dreams and memories to see Ryan Goleen again.

It was ten at night. Lucy was almost ready for bed, but she couldn't pull away from the photo on the computer screen.

She was looking at the award ceremony from two years

ago, the one in which God had first showed her Christian Windsor. The picture had Christian in it, but he wasn't the focus. No, that had been given to Luke Titan, as if *he* was special.

Lucy didn't like someone taking the spotlight from Christian one bit.

Could she get to Titan? Sacrifice him for the Lord? For Christian?

A silly question. Of course she could. God was on her side, after all.

Lucy logged off the computer and walked across the campus to her bedroom. She was being given more and more privileges. All the staff agreed she was a model resident. She'd be free from this place soon, and then she could pick up the pace. The Lord's work wasn't to be put off, after all.

She lay down in bed, but instead of hoping for another dream, she thought about Luke Titan. He was tall, and Lucy thought a lot could be done with that.

The Bible had many lessons on how best to hurt people.

# CHAPTER TEN

Night had fallen three hours ago and Christian's mother was sleeping. Christian couldn't fall asleep, and he knew why. His earlier conversation with Tommy. They'd spoken after Luke dropped Christian back off at his mother's. Their conversation had been simple.

*Firm* was another way to describe it.

"I don't know how your mind works, Christian," Tommy said, "but I know what you did with Brown. I know that you got us inside that house at exactly the right time before he killed innocent people. I know that you figured out his life story without ever meeting the man. All this guilt bullshit you're feeling. It's keeping you from stopping *this* person, which means he'll kill again. What if it's me, Christian? Or Luke? Or your mom? Whoever he is, you're letting him continue by not going inside your head."

Christian hadn't said anything after the spiel.

"Are you there?" Tommy asked.

"I have to go," he had said, then hung up.

Now, three hours later, he still hadn't done what Tommy suggested.

To go inside himself, to his mansion, would mean that he'd have to understand this person—this murderer—and he didn't want to. At all. Brown had been different. It wasn't personal, even in the end. Now, though, this pseudo-priest had *made* it personal.

"Just shut up," he said. "Just shut up with your excuses."

The Priest was probably stalking his next victim. Deciding who would be sacrificed for the great Christian Windsor.

Christian closed his eyes.

---

When he opened them, he stood at a door that was right next to Bradley Brown's room. He looked over at the older room and saw that where *The Surgeon* had once been written at the top, it now simply read the man's name.

Dust rested at the bottom of the door. Christian hadn't gone inside that room for a long time. He didn't know if he ever would again.

Christian's mind mansion was a glorious structure that housed every aspect of his life, categorizing everything and allowing him access at any time. He'd created this place involuntarily as a boy who needed a sanctuary where he could hide and deal with the intense intelligence gifted him. The corridors stretched on endlessly, his mind constantly creating new rooms and hallways as needed. His brain never bothered him with the construction or categorization, but simply let him come and go as he needed.

The room he stood outside had the exact same door and frame as Bradley's, but different words were carved in the marble above the doorway: *The Priest*.

Blood dripped from the letters' grooves, reaching the top of the doorframe where it pooled before spilling over, finding its final resting place in front of Christian's feet.

Christian knew the blood was a representation of his guilt.

He swallowed, reached for the door handle, and stepped over the small puddle.

Christian went inside the room he'd been avoiding. His eyes narrowed as he took in his mind's new creation. A circle of statues filled the middle of the room. Concrete, and life-sized. All were bowing down, and all had blood dripping from the holes in their faces where there should be eyes, ears, noses, and mouths. Some wore shrouds, others were in the act of ripping out their hair, and some were merely praying.

All were bleeding, and all of them knelt before the statue of Christian that stood in the middle of their circle.

The stone replica of himself was smiling. His hands were in front of him, the palms turned up and blood dripping from them. The drips hit the floor beneath with sickening smacks, as if each droplet weighed far more than it should.

Christian stepped closer, looking at the maniacal grin across his stone face. "What is this?"

The vents above turned on and Christian looked up. He hadn't turned them on, yet the air was pumping out.

"You don't like it?" a voice hissed from the vent.

Christian took a step backward, still looking up but unconsciously putting distance between himself and the statue. He didn't recognize the voice, only that it wasn't his. Nothing had ever spoken to him in here before. This place was his, and his alone, and yet...

"It's okay, Christian. You've been inviting me here for a long time. I'm surprised you didn't know."

Christian's mouth was slightly ajar but he said nothing. He wouldn't speak to it. Whatever it was, it shouldn't be here.

"What do you think about the statues in front of you? I watched your mind build them, but I'm not sure if I had any influence over it. I'd like to think I did."

Christian shook his head. He couldn't see anything inside the vent, but the voice came from it all the same.

"Cat got your tongue?" it asked. "It's okay, Christian. There's no need to be frightened. You and I, we're the same. You might not see it yet, but you will."

Christian had backed up so far that he slammed into the closed door. His hands desperately searched for the handle behind him.

"What about what Tommy said? Shouldn't you stay here so you can find out who is doing all this killing? Look at the statue. What do you see?"

Christian did as he was told. Blood now pooled in the statue's eyes before rolling down its cheeks and forming red rivers.

"You don't like it?"

Christian couldn't breathe. His chest locked up, and he was unable to suck in air.

"Go on, then. Leave if you don't like this place. I do. I think I'll stay."

Christian fled the mansion he'd spent years building.

When he opened his eyes back in his mother's house, the sweat had soaked through his shirt and he couldn't stop panting.

# THE BOOK OF LAMENTATIONS

# CHAPTER ELEVEN

*Six months later*

The case slowly went cold and for Christian, it was a relief. He didn't dare venture back into his mansion during that time. His mind still worked just as fast, although his insight was diminished because of it. That was fine with him, as long as he didn't hear that voice whispering from vents above his head.

He hadn't told Melissa about it. Neither did he tell his mother or his partners. When the murders stopped, Luke and Tommy had quit demanding that he go inside himself, and so Christian allowed what happened to slip away.

He didn't want to face it, even if that meant never entering his sanctuary again. That voice and those statues... Maybe the room would disappear in time. Maybe the voice would die. Christian stayed away, fearing for his very sanity.

The FBI didn't close the Priest's file, but the three partners had to let it grow cold as more cases came in.

Christian did his best to push what happened to Ryan

Goleen from his head. He tried not to think about Mrs. Brown and the cross carved into her face.

Tommy attacked his work as usual while making a home for him and Alice. He wanted to marry her and was thinking about proposing in the next few months. He saved money each paycheck for exactly that.

Luke was, perhaps, the only one who still consciously thought about the Priest and the case they no longer actively worked. He still saw an opening for himself, and regardless of what Tommy and Christian said, he knew it wasn't over. The Priest, or Priestess as he'd grown convinced was the correct term, would return. Luke wasn't sure why she'd left, only that unless she was dead, her devotion hadn't ended.

———

For Lucy Speckle, those six months were some of the most arduous of her life. She thought about little else than moving forward with the sacrifices, but it would have been too hard. Too risky. Keeping Ryan Goleen tied up and hanging in the air for multiple days, all the while hoping that no one would hear his screams was difficult enough.

No, God's plans shouldn't be put off, but they also shouldn't be rushed.

So Lucy continued planning, but she stopped acting on her plans. She kept her appointments with Dr. Brigham, and he kept telling her how much she was progressing. She smiled at the right spots and even started speaking a bit more, although the stuttering still plagued her at every chance.

Finally, six months or so after she had mailed the video of Ryan Goleen's glorious death, Lucy Speckle was cleared to leave the halfway house.

She had an apartment already lined up, and she'd been given a raise at her job. She was making twelve dollars an hour now, more than she'd ever been paid before. She put everything she owned in one suitcase, carrying it in her right hand, and in her left, she carried the Bible.

Lucy actually owned a few more things, but those were in a bat bag, hidden inside a storage unit thirty miles from the halfway house.

Lucy got into her father's old car and drove it straight to her apartment.

It wasn't furnished, or in a nice part of town, but the doors locked and the price was right.

She parked her car and looked at her new home. Mexican kids played on the lawn in front of the apartments. She heard their laughter and then heard it stop as they looked at the new white lady. The right side of Lucy's lip twitched rapidly.

She didn't notice. She didn't care that the kids were staring at her, either. There had been a time when something like that would have enraged her, but now that she saw things clearly, she realized they were nonessential. The people that had mocked her had never been essential.

Lucy already had her key and she walked up the stairs to the second floor. She found apartment 246 and opened the door.

As she stepped inside, she realized that there was a lot of work to do. Not just for Christian, but for this place, too. Cleanliness was next to Godliness, and this apartment had been neglected for far too long. She could smell it, the filth from its last inhabitants. Drug addicts, probably. Perhaps even worse, homosexuals or pedophiles.

That was okay. Lucy was a hard worker and she was ready to get to the Lord's business. Her absence from it had gone on long enough.

---

School had been a chore for Lucy.

"If you'd stop soundin' like a damn retard, you wouldn't have no problems," her daddy told her.

It grew worse and worse, reaching a climax when she was around eleven years old.

Each year, Lucy went to her teachers and requested to sit at the back of the class. Most years, the teachers let her. They knew who Lucy Speckle was—and who her daddy was—and what church they attended. It was a small town of only a few thousand people, and the thirty or so crazies who went to Pastor Martin's church once a week were ostracized from everyone else.

So why not put the little freak at the back of the class? After all, the teachers didn't want problems in their class-rooms. They wanted to teach their lessons and make it home without having to say "Sit down and be quiet" too many times.

When Lucy was eleven Mrs. Treadwell told her that she would prefer it if Lucy sat in the front. Lucy had stared at her, not knowing *what* to say. She hadn't thought this a possibility, given that every other teacher hadn't made a big deal of the request.

So the year began with Lucy sitting front and center.

Mrs. Treadwell, for her part, probably thought she was doing the girl a favor by trying to bring her out from the shadows and letting the other kids get to know her better.

The twitching started around this time.

Mrs. Treadwell certainly shouldn't be *blamed* for it, but the stress from moving to the front of the class was a definite catalyst. Lucy's eyebrows started hopping on her face like crickets, and her mouth twitched and jerked as if invisible hooks were attached to her lips and pulling constantly.

*"Freak!"* one of the girls yelled after school. Her name was Terry, but Lucy forgot it as she grew older. She never forgot the sound Terry made, though, or the way she screamed as if Lucy was a demon sprung from hell. As if she was *evil.*

Lucy cried that day as she walked home, clutching her Bible to her chest. She wore a book bag for the rest of her books, but the Bible she wanted close for comfort.

"Hey, freak!" a boy taunted. "Your daddy beatin' your momma still?"

Lucy squinted and looked ahead, trying to keep the tears from falling down her face. The kids were behind her, but she didn't want to chance them seeing her crying.

Lucy didn't know who launched the first rock. She only knew it felt like her arm exploded when it collided with her shoulder. Her Bible dropped to the ground, its thin pages opening up and scraping across the concrete.

"The freak dropped her Bible!" someone screamed.

Another rock hit the ground right in front of Lucy.

She didn't know what to do. She saw the Bible lying there disrespected, but she heard another rock land just behind her. It shattered and tiny pebbles cascaded against her ankles. Her right arm blazed with pain and tears blurred her vision.

Lucy took off. Her right arm felt dead, and she couldn't use it to help pump her legs faster, but she kept running as fast as she could.

She ran the whole mile and a half, bursting through the front door and into the living room. She was hyperventilating, unable to stop her lungs from craving air, while the rest of her body only wanted to sob. She fell to her knees and started dry heaving on the floor.

She didn't see her father walk in from the kitchen. Her mother remained at the table, not looking up from whatever task was before her.

Lucy continued nearly retching for a full minute, and then, completely exhausted, she collapsed to the floor.

"Where's your Bible?" Daddy asked.

Lucy let out a cry, shame and guilt washing over her as surely as it had Jesus when he donned both the cross and mankind's sin.

"Daddy, Daddy, they were throwing rocks."

"I said, where is your Bible?"

"At school," she whispered.

"Well, get up. Let's go get it."

Lucy looked at her father, hoping that he was joking, but knowing even as she searched for a hint of humor, she'd find nothing.

They got into Daddy's pickup and drove toward the school. They were two hundred feet off when her father stopped the truck.

"That your Bible?"

Lucy said nothing. What could she do?

The thin sheets of the Lord's scripture were flying down the street like tiny magic carpets, the wind blowing them this way and that. She saw the leather binding lying about twenty feet from where she dropped it. It looked empty, like a silo after all the corn had been sold.

*That's what you did. You sold out God. Like Judas.*

Her father turned and looked at her, his gaze the same as the Lord's for all Lucy cared. He cast the same judgment and she knew that penance would be hard.

"Well get out and go get 'em," Daddy said.

More tears filled her eyes but she didn't dare return Daddy's stare. She got out of the truck and started chasing down the flying papers. Her father sat and watched. Finally, two hours after dusk, Lucy had collected every page that was still on the street, though she knew some had flown far, far off.

She brought them all back to Daddy's truck.

"All right. Now you go home and put 'em all back in that leather binding. Tomorrow we'll deal with penance."

# CHAPTER TWELVE

"So, are you going to write a book on me?" Christian asked, smiling.

Veronica smiled back. "When did he tell you?"

"The first day you called. Luke said he thought it would be good for both of us. You know, you have to tell me if you're going to. Or maybe you don't *have* to, but you should."

Christian and Veronica sat outside on an unusually warm day for November. Christian had a Coke and Veronica had ordered a martini. They had done this once a week for the past six months, with thankfully few interruptions from complex cases. Every Friday, they met after work for drinks and dinner. Veronica insisted they switch the place every Friday.

Christian *hated* that.

"You know why she's doing it, right?" his psychiatrist had asked.

"Why?"

"Same reason I make you talk about things you don't want to in here. Because it stretches you. It's good for you."

So he went every Friday to whatever new place she picked. Christian, despite what he originally thought, truly looked forward to their dinners. Veronica was funny and she laughed at what he said, although she told him she didn't know if he was joking half the time.

When he told his mother about it, she only said, "Really? That's nice."

Which had been a bit surprising at first, but Christian finally understood his mother was simply playing a role. Making a big deal out of it would increase Christian's anxiety, ruining the whole experience. He *definitely* didn't want that to happen.

"I'm thinking about it," Veronica said, answering his question about whether she'd actually write a book on him.

"You'll kill your career. No one is going to read it. I'm boring."

"You are." She smiled again. "But you're also interesting in a sly way."

Christian took a sip from his drink and let the breeze blow across him. "How's your therapy going?"

"I'm not sure I'll ever get used to your bluntness."

"That's not an answer to the question." Christian was finding himself more and more comfortable around her. He liked that as well, the ability to be himself without too much fear.

"It's good. Luke actually asked me the same question the other day, whether or not I'd be writing a book. My honest opinion is that it's too early. I think maybe when you're forty, there will be enough accolades under your belt to really sell some copies."

"So does that mean we won't be meeting anymore?"

"I can't tell if you're serious."

"Kind of."

"No. I'm writing more now, and I think you're probably part of the reason. Maybe you're becoming my muse."

Christian looked away, nodding. Not for the first time, he wondered if he *liked* Veronica. Romantically. It was an odd thing for him to contemplate since it had never come up with another woman. He'd been attracted to women, but this was the first time that he'd, well, longed for someone's presence other than his mother's.

"I think I like you." He didn't look at her as he said it.

"I think I like you, too," Veronica said, her eyes directly on him.

"I don't know what you do when you like someone. I've never had it happen before."

Veronica smiled but didn't waste time. She stood up and walked to his side of the table.

He looked up, his eyes wide as she bent down and kissed him on the lips.

---

Luke never gave any thought to how the world would judge his actions. If he had, his life would have turned out very, very differently. Some of the things he did would obviously be considered criminal, while others would only be seen as creepy.

One Friday evening, as the sun was just about ready to

set, Luke sat in his car and watched Veronica Lopez kiss Christian Windsor.

Mr. Windsor and Ms. Lopez. A couple, finally.

He'd been following them for the last five months. Since they'd gotten their Friday date ritual down. He was waiting for this moment, the one where their mutual attraction finally overflowed.

Most people wouldn't think Ms. Lopez would fall for someone like Mr. Windsor, but Luke knew differently. His partner was odd, but something about him caused you to fall in love with him. His fragility. His honesty. His raw intelligence.

Luke was planning on using the two of them, especially now that they were an item.

But first, he needed to deal with the Priestess.

He had spotted her a week ago, although he hadn't been completely sure it was the correct woman. Her gait gave it away. She walked as she had in the video, as if her bones and ligaments weren't connected exactly right. Luke knew that wasn't the case. Most likely, she suffered from a neurological malady. Her brain sent out electrical pulses at the wrong time, causing the jerky movements.

She didn't know Luke had spotted her. She was following him. He had to give her some credit. She was decent at remaining unnoticed. Probably something she picked up throughout her life.

Right now, while Luke watched Christian, the Priestess was watching him. She wasn't in a car this time. She was waiting at a bus stop down the street. Her face kept twitching as she pretended to read the magazine on her lap.

She wanted *him* this time. What did she have planned? Was she going to serve him up as another sacrifice for her God?

More importantly, what did Luke want to do about it?

---

Luke got into bed that night and waited for the Priestess to arrive. He wore a robe and rested on top of his comforter, staring straight up at the ceiling as he listened for her. He didn't strain to hear everything happening around him. He easily picked up the smallest noise, even from outside the house. She'd been following him for a week, but today was the closest she'd gotten to him.

He had no alarm system in his house, perhaps his most egregious sign of arrogance. Luke wondered if she planned to disarm any alarms, or if she would improvise on arriving. She wouldn't need to work hard to find him. He was excited at the opportunity.

At twelve-thirty, Luke heard her. The sound was faint, even for his ears, but he knew she was scaling the fence outside. A strong woman, just as the video showed. He'd heard no car pass, which was curious, but he figured there would be time to understand how she had traveled later.

He remained in bed, losing her for a second as she ran across the lawn.

Then she was there again, at his back door. He had left it unlocked, and the smart girl turned the knob before trying to break in.

It opened easily.

Luke listened as she made her way through the house,

checking each of the rooms for signs of her prize. Then the moon cast her shadow across his room.

Luke saw her nearly perfectly, his night vision more like a jungle cat's than a human's.

*How well can* you *see?* he wondered.

The Priestess didn't reach for the light switch. She didn't move at all as she looked at him.

"Yuh-You're awake?"

Luke smiled, the moonlight gleaming off his teeth. "Yes."

"You were waiting on me?"

"Yes."

She turned her face and looked out his bedroom window, seeing the vast expanse of his lawn. He knew she was considering running. She hadn't figured Luke would be ready. After a second, she looked back at him.

Luke watched her come, impressed with her speed and strength. He let himself fall into the Priestess' darkness without a cry.

# CHAPTER THIRTEEN

Tommy looked across the floor at Luke's office. He glanced at his watch, then returned to staring at the empty room.

It was noon and Luke was nowhere to be seen.

Tommy stepped out of his own office and took the corridor down to Christian, not bothering to knock as he entered.

"Have you heard from Luke?"

Christian, for maybe the first time, wasn't staring at his screen with the intensity it would take to crack Russia's nuclear arsenal. He sat with his chair turned around, looking out the office window. They were only on the third floor, but it wasn't the worst view in the world.

"Luke? He's not in his office?" Christian said, not turning around.

"No, genius. That's why I'm down here. Has he called you?"

Christian shook his head.

"He's not answering his phone."

Christian didn't move.

"Hello? Earth to Christian? Are you listening to me at all?"

Finally, the kid swiveled his chair. "Alice is your girl-friend, right?"

"What? What are you talking about? I'm saying Luke isn't here and he isn't answering his phone. Why are you asking about Alice?"

"How did you know she was your girlfriend, like when it first happened?"

Tommy stepped farther into the office and closed the door behind him. "Hey, man. Are you okay?"

Christian nodded.

"Then if that's true, I need you to focus on what I'm saying. We need to go to Luke's house and see where the hell he is."

"Okay," Christian said. He stood up, grabbed his jacket, and walked past Tommy.

"The hell?" Tommy whispered as Christian left the office. He wasn't sure he'd ever seen Christian with such a carefree attitude, *especially* not with a possible problem arising. Sure, Luke being late to work wasn't the advent of World War III, but it also wasn't something that *happened*. It wasn't like him to not answer his cell either.

Tommy didn't like it.

He followed Christian to the elevator and stepped in beside him. Other people were riding down as well, so Tommy remained quiet until they stepped off and exited the building.

"What's going on with you?"

"I think I might have a girlfriend," Christian said.

Tommy stopped, a smile coming over his face despite Luke's absence. "You serious? Someone wants to date you?"

"She kissed me."

"Jesus. What's her name?"

"You won't believe me."

"Let me hear it," Tommy said.

"It's Veronica."

"Lopez?"

Christian nodded.

Tommy stared for a few more seconds and then started walking to his car. "You're right. I don't believe it."

They both climbed into Tommy's vehicle and he started toward Luke's house.

"So she kissed you, huh?"

"Yeah, on Friday."

"Have you called her since?"

Christian shook his head.

"You're kidding."

"No. We don't call each other until Friday afternoon."

"Oh, dear God," Tommy said, unable to stop smiling. "Was that your first kiss?"

"Yes."

He sighed. "That changes things. You need to call her as soon as possible. You don't kiss a woman and then go a whole weekend without communicating with her. It sends the signal that you're not interested." He looked at Christian. Terror had grown across his face like a weed. "Hey, calm down. If she's into you enough to kiss you, then she's gotta know you're a weird guy. I'm sure she knows you like her. I'd just give her a call tonight if I were you."

They arrived at Luke's house about twenty minutes

later. The gate was closed, so Tommy rolled his window down and pressed the buzzer.

No answer.

"I don't feel good about this," he said. He looked at Christian, the kid finally focusing on something other than his new girlfriend.

"Me either," Christian said.

Tommy left the keys in the car and stepped out. Christian followed from the passenger's side. Tommy saw no movement inside the home, and the curtains were all open, giving him a good view of the interior. Luke was nowhere to be seen.

"We need to get inside," Christian said.

"What are you thinking?" Tommy trusted the kid's instincts, perhaps even more than Luke's. Certainly more than his own, and he trusted himself a whole hell of a lot. Right now, *his* instincts said something was very wrong here.

"His car's gone." Christian pointed at the empty driveway.

Tommy stepped forward and pulled on the gate. It was a single structure that slid in only one direction. There wasn't a split in the middle where the two might have been able to squeeze through. The gate didn't move at all.

"All right, I'm going to pull my car up. We'll get on the front bumper and I'll shove you over the top. I'll come after."

They did as he suggested, and Tommy landed hard on the other side of the fence, rattling his knees. He was too heavy for these acrobatics.

"You need to exercise more," Christian said without looking at him.

"I had to throw your ass over."

They went to the front door, but they didn't even have to twist the knob. It stood slightly ajar. Tommy said nothing, but flipped the latch on his holster and pulled his gun out.

Christian did the same.

They walked through the house, clearing each room, neither saying anything. If Luke was here, he would know who was in his house. If anyone else had entered, then Tommy didn't want to alert them.

The two reached Luke's room.

Tommy pulled his cellphone out, and without thinking, dialed 9-1-1.

"This is Special Agent Thomas Phillips with the FBI. We have a missing agent, Luke Titan. House location: 1946 Trinity Lane."

He listened as the dispatcher asked questions, staring at the dried blood across Luke's white pillowcase.

# CHAPTER FOURTEEN

Luke opened his eyes. He'd been conscious for some time, but his head hurt and he had known light would intensify the pain.

The Priestess had arrived, and she deserved an audience.

He was in the same metal prison where Ryan Goleen had met his end.

A woman stood in front of Luke. Her hair was long and scraggly. She was a skinny thing. Luke hadn't forgotten how easily she scaled his fence the previous night. Skinny she may be, but lacking muscle she wasn't. Her eyes were brown. She wore a white t-shirt and a pair of jeans that looked like she needed another twenty pounds just to hold them up.

"A pleasure, I'm sure," Luke said. He didn't wince, though the overhead light caused pain to flare inside his head.

"Huh-how did you know I would be there last night?" the woman asked, her lips barely moving as she spoke, like if she opened her mouth too wide, all her words might simply spill out, leaving her unable to speak.

"I saw you watching me."

"When?"

"Quite a few times, actually. I'd venture to say all of them."

The Priestess said nothing as she stood in front of Luke. She stared at him as if measuring his words for their weight in truth.

"Thuh-thuh-there's something wrong with you," she said after a moment.

"Isn't that true for all of us?"

The woman shook her head, but Luke knew she wasn't answering him. She saw Luke, but that shake was for her. She stared for another second and then turned around. She pulled open the metal door easily, enough for her to bend and slip underneath it. Luke watched as it closed. He heard a lock hit home outside.

He didn't make a single noise, just closed his eyes again to block out the bright lights from above.

This was going to be very, very interesting.

---

Lucy didn't go home.

She walked to the car that she'd driven here, the one that had been sitting in Titan's driveway. She'd taken it last night after throwing him in the trunk. Hers was parked in a ditch off a main road five miles away from Titan's house. Lucy had thought she might have to carry the man back, but she'd ended up taking his car instead.

A dangerous move if someone were to have seen it, but Lucy couldn't worry about that right now. She was too concerned with Luke Titan.

Lucy sat on the hood of the hundred-thousand-dollar car with no thought of its value.

The man inside the storage unit was very different than she'd expected. Lucy wasn't sure exactly what to do, only that she didn't like being around him. Lucy had never been frightened of anyone in this life, besides her father. When he'd died, Lucy had no need to fear anyone anymore. Everything he'd taught her had stuck. God was the only one deserving of fear.

Yet, when she looked at the man inside the storage unit, she *felt* fear.

Real and horrible, like with her father when she was younger. Fear that the man could hurt her in indescribable ways. Perhaps even ways that would damn her eternal soul, however silly that sounded. She'd given her soul to Christ and no one could take it from *Him*.

Yet, she didn't want to go back in there.

Was he the Devil, or a demon? If so, what was Lucy supposed to do?

She closed her eyes and ground her teeth together until her jaw creaked.

God wasn't answering. He shared not a single word of what her next steps should be.

Lucy was alone with the Devil. She couldn't stop, couldn't let that evil thing keep her from her purpose, which was to bring Christian Windsor forward.

No wonder this evil creature had taken glory from

Christian. He'd been trying to steal glory from God on high since the dawn of time.

"Give me the strength to do what needs to be done. In Jesus' name. Amen."

She stood back from the car and pulled the padlock key from her pocket. Lucy walked back to the storage unit and went inside, intent on sacrificing this demon for her Lord and her soon-to-be-savior, Christian.

———

"That was fast," Luke said.

"Hush, serpent."

Luke wanted to smile but knew that would be foolish.

"Christian Windsor, is he the Second Coming?"

"Get thee behind me, Satan," the woman said. She moved past Luke's chair, but he didn't turn to look at her as she grabbed something.

"What do you plan to do with me?"

"What the Lord was too gracious to do five thousand years ago."

The Priestess laid a bag down ten feet in front of Luke, then went behind him again. She dragged a long piece of wood across the floor, laid it next to the bag, then went back to the well of gifts resting at the back of the unit.

She brought another piece of wood forward, followed by a bucket, and then a large sack of cement mix.

"Oh, that's good," Luke said, seriously impressed. "You strung Mr. Goleen up, but you're actually going to crucify me. Is that right?"

"Something like that, serpent. But, you won't go as my Lord did. I think I'll crucify you upside down."

"You truly are your master's servant," Luke said.

"We are all the Lord's servants." The woman bent over the bag, pulling out tools. Clearly, she had thought this through. She pulled out twelve-inch metal nails, as well as a large hammer.

"You'll want to be careful not to split the wood when you put those in," Luke said. "It might be more difficult than you imagine. How are you planning on going about it?"

She said nothing.

"It would be easiest if you were to nail the wood together, then with the cross lying inside the bucket, harden the cement. You can nail me to it after. I promise not to struggle."

The Priestess looked up, her eyebrows twitching rapidly and her mouth twisted in an awful snarl. "Sh-shut your mouth, or I'll cut your tongue out."

Luke nodded and remained silent as the woman placed one piece of wood over the other.

"If you go through with this right now, you'll waste a grand opportunity," he said as she lifted the hammer above the nail. She stopped mid-swing but didn't look at him. "What better way could you honor Christian, than to have his mother watch my death?"

Slowly, the Priestess tilted her face up. Her eyebrows were still and her lips pressed into a thin line.

"I can tell you where she lives, and you can bring her here. She can witness what you're doing for her son."

# CHAPTER FIFTEEN

Christian stood in Luke's bedroom as FBI techs worked around him. Tommy was in the living room, answering questions for investigators. They would come to him next, Christian knew, and he didn't want to consider the answers he'd have for them.

*It's not the Priest*, he thought as he stared at one of the techs slowly removing the pillow from its case. The blood covering it was curved like a smile as if it was laughing at him with dark, red lipstick.

*It's not the Priest.*

Six months ago felt like a lifetime, yet Christian was realizing how foolish he'd been. How foolish they had all been, acting as though the nightmare was over just because the murders stopped. He'd gone on with his life, ignoring everything that had happened. Ignoring the promise he made to a grieving woman. Ignoring the fact that he could no longer venture inside his mansion because he was too goddamn scared.

Luke and Tommy had gone along with it because the cases kept coming in.

Christian had gone along with it because he couldn't stand the *truth*. Someone was murdering people because of him.

Maybe his mother was right. Maybe that didn't make him guilty. But facts were still facts, and Luke's blood now shouted them from that pillowcase.

"Christian?" Tommy called. He was standing next to a young, black man. "This is Agent Bench. He'll be working with us on this."

"Call me Perry," the agent said. "Can we talk for a few minutes?"

Christian nodded and walked out of Luke's bedroom.

They went to the living room and sat on separate couches. Christian had sat here countless times with Luke. Not now, though.

"I want to let you know that this is personal for me," Perry said. "I don't know Dr. Titan, but that doesn't matter. He's one of us."

Christian nodded, hearing the man but not caring what he said.

"When was your last conversation with Dr. Titan?"

"Last Friday."

"Do you mind recounting what was said?"

Christian went through the questions on autopilot, his mind feeding him answers.

Finally, the agent stood and shook his hand, then walked off. Christian stared at the coffee table. He didn't look up when Tommy approached and sat next to him.

"I've heard of Bench. He's a solid agent. I just got off the phone with Waverly. He's mobilizing everything within his power. We'll find him."

"Six months ago," Christian told him, not entirely sure where he'd finish but knowing it was important to tell someone, "I went into my mansion. I wanted to look at the Priest. Understand him and what he wanted. Something was waiting for me, though. Something foreign. There shouldn't be anything in there, Tommy. Not in my head, not in that place. I haven't gone back in, and the murders stopped so I haven't needed to use it since."

Tommy was quiet. Christian understood that Tommy didn't fully grasp what he was saying. Hell, maybe Christian didn't, either.

"I don't want to go back in there now, but that room is waiting for me. The voice, too. Whatever it is, it's still there."

"Christian," Tommy said, "I need you to be a little more concise with what you're saying. It's not making much sense."

Christian looked up from the coffee table. "The Priest did this, and if I don't go back inside my mansion, Luke's going to die. But, if I do go back, I'm afraid I'll lose my mind."

---

Patricia Windsor was washing dishes when the person called the Priest came for her. She enjoyed washing dishes. There was a meditative quality to it.

She usually did it in the afternoon when the sun was starting its descent and shining in through the kitchen window. When it was warm out, she'd open the window and soak up some of the rays.

Today, she wasn't finding her normal peace in the chore. Patricia was worrying about her son.

When he was around, she never showed a single ounce of worry. Since he was a toddler, she'd known it was necessary for her to always look confident in what she did. It was necessary for his sake that she hide any feelings of fear.

However, Patricia wasn't a superhero, and she worried just like anyone else. Now, with much of her life behind her, she worried more and more about her son.

He hadn't called yesterday, and that was unusual. Nothing to panic about. She understood his job was demanding in a way that others weren't. Still, it was mid-afternoon and she hadn't heard from him yet.

"Why don't you just call him, then?" she said to the empty kitchen.

Not a bad idea, and something she probably should have done hours ago, rather than stand here and ruin a perfectly good dishwashing session.

She reached below to the cabinet's door handle and pulled the dishrag off it to dry her hands. Patricia walked into her living room and picked up the portable telephone. She sat down on the couch and dialed Christian's cell.

That was when she noticed the woman standing in her house. She stood in the left corner, just beside the television that Christian had bought her for her last birthday.

Patricia hung up the phone and slowly set it down next to her. She lifted her head up in the same deliberate manner until her eyes fell on the woman.

A thin thing, with hair that looked closer to pine straw

than actual hair. She held a knife in her right hand and a large roll of duct tape in her left. Patricia felt adrenaline pour into her veins, but she didn't move. As she'd done with her son for so many years, she showed nothing of the turmoil inside her.

"I don't want to hurt you," the woman said.

"Okay."

"I need you to come with me. It's about your son. I want to shu-show you suh-something."

The woman's mouth twitched as she spoke, the corner of her lip looking like it wanted to pull back and touch her ear.

"I'll come with you," Patricia said. "You don't have to hurt me or my son."

The woman's head cocked sideways. Her eyebrows started dancing just like the corner of her lip.

"Hurt your son? I'd *never* hurt him. I'll only hurt you if you try to hurt him, Mrs. Windsor."

Patricia said a small prayer as the thin woman walked toward her. She closed her eyes, hoping the panic she'd kept at bay for Christian's sake wouldn't now rise.

---

"I-I'm sorry about this," Lucy said, and she was. She didn't like doing it, but she also couldn't let Mrs. Windsor sit in the passenger seat. Christian's mother was in the back, her wrists and ankles taped together.

Lucy couldn't bring herself to tape the woman's mouth shut, not given her place in the Lord's plan. She was, after all, Christian Windsor's mother.

A black pillowcase rested over her head, and Lucy had asked her to lie down across the backseat, which she'd done without any hesitation.

Lucy liked her, as she'd thought she would. She hated that she'd brought the freaking knife. She just didn't know what else to do. Lucy was beginning to doubt what the demon had told her to do, although it made so much sense at the time.

*It makes sense now*, she thought. *His mother needs to see what Christian's becoming. He will love that you involved her.*

While that might be true, God had said nothing on the matter.

She had to work tomorrow and she wasn't sure what to do with Mrs. Windsor. She didn't want to tie her up in the storage unit. That was no way to treat someone of such high status.

*Oh goodness*, Lucy thought. *God, I need your help here.*

She parked the car outside the storage unit.

"I-I'll b-be right back. Puh-puh-please don't luh-luh-leave."

Her stuttering was getting worse. A definite sign she shouldn't have done this. The demon was tricking her. Lucy got out of the car and unlocked the unit's door, slipping underneath as usual.

"Y-y-you're not to talk to me anymore!" she shouted.

The man still sat in the chair. His lip was swollen as was his left eye, but he smiled despite the pain he must have felt.

"Did you get Christian's mother?"

Lucy's head jerked to the side, fast and hard, then just as

115

quickly jerked back to looking at the demon. She didn't notice.

"S-s-s-shhh." Lucy paused and thought about the word she wanted to pronounce. "Sshheee's in the car."

"Good. That's important for what you're about to create. Are you going to bring her in here?"

Lucy felt lost. She had come in here wanting the demon to shut up but now he was trying to help her? Her head jerked the opposite way as if someone had slapped her. It snapped back forward just as fast. "Nuh-no. I'm not putting huh-her next to you."

The man nodded. Lucy kept finding herself drawn to his eyes, even with one of them swelling. "Where will you keep her?" he asked.

"At my place." She didn't know why she was answering him, or even why she was still here. Why she had come to begin with.

"Are you sure that's wise? Here, it's unlikely someone will find her."

"*Shut up!*"

The man did as she said.

Lucy needed to think. She didn't want to leave the woman with this hell-sent creature. But if she did bring Christian's mother home… God helped those who helped themselves. If she did something stupid in His service, He might find her unworthy.

"I'm sure you'll figure out the correct path, but there's one more person I think you may want here when you crucify me."

"Who?"

"Her name is Veronica Lopez. She and Christian are beginning a romantic relationship."

Lucy felt the air leave her lungs as if someone had slugged her in the stomach.

"She's an atheist," Titan said. "She doesn't believe in God."

Lucy could barely believe it. This hadn't been part of the plan. Christian Windsor had a heathen girlfriend? That wasn't what God wanted, and it sure as *hell* wasn't what Lucy wanted.

Her face danced in different rhythms, creating something truly frightening.

"I-I-I-I'll be back."

# CHAPTER SIXTEEN

"Thanks for seeing me," Christian said.

"Of course," Melissa said from her chair. "What's going on?"

"We haven't released anything to the news yet, but Luke's been kidnapped."

Christian watched Melissa's eyes widen. "Your partner?"

He nodded.

"You're sure he was actually kidnapped? He didn't just, I don't know, leave?"

"There was blood in his house, but there didn't appear to be a struggle."

"Does that make sense to you?"

Christian shook his head but said nothing else.

"What brought you in today? Was it Luke, or something else?" Melissa asked.

"You're good at your job, you know that? You're perceptive."

"So are you."

"In a different way," Christian said. He leaned back in the chair and stared out the window in front of him. After a few seconds, he said, "I haven't told you about this because I'm too scared to really talk about it. I haven't gone to my mansion in six months. The last time I was there, something was waiting for me."

"Something?"

"Yes. A voice."

"What did it say?" she asked.

"That it liked the mansion. That it wanted to stay."

"That place is yours, Christian. Whatever is in there, it's simply a part of you. It's not something foreign or separate."

"*That* wasn't part of me," he said. "It's someone else. Something else. It shouldn't be there."

His psychiatrist nodded for a few seconds and then said, "Think about this logically. What's inside your head is simply a way to categorize how you see the world. Nothing else. If something in there is talking to you, it's not a supernatural being. It's your mind categorizing something you've experienced, but maybe in a way you don't recognize."

"The thing is, I have to go back in there. The Priest took Luke, at least I think so. Luke believed the person was creating sacrifices for me, and now *he's* going to be the sacrifice. If I don't go back into the mansion, I won't... I won't be able to stop him."

"What do you think will happen if you turn inward?" Melissa asked.

"I might lose my mind."

"What did you see when you were in there last?"

He shook his head, not wanting to remember the scene inside that room. He hadn't thought about it in months, not until he saw the blood on Luke's pillow.

"You can talk about it, Christian. It's not going to hurt you."

"There were statues. All of them kneeling before a statue of me, and my statue stood in the middle with its hands out and palms up. Blood was dripping off the palms, and it was smiling. That's not how any other room is organized, Melissa. The rest of them are like you said, categorizing and arranging the outside world so that I can examine it when I want. This was saying something about me. It wasn't a categorization, but a prediction."

"I'm not sure that's true." Melissa paused and Christian looked from the window to her. "It's fear, Christian. Do you *know* these are sacrifices to you for sure? I mean, is there any real evidence to point in that direction besides Luke's suggestion?"

"There's not much evidence at all, on anything the Priest has done."

"So, maybe your mind created what Luke said was happening. Maybe your fear made what's in that room. Perhaps you should go back and see if anything is different."

Christian gritted his teeth. "I *have* to go back. I don't have a fucking choice. Luke's time is running out by the second. I shouldn't even be here. I should be at the office right now." He looked up at the clock on the wall. "It's ten at night, and I know Tommy is there. He's working the case, and I'm here talking about my fucking feelings."

"It's a big improvement, Christian. When you started coming here, you couldn't express anything out loud."

"I don't need improvements right now. I need to save Luke."

---

Tommy watched Christian walk across the office floor, the lights above him dark. He moved like a shadow, quiet, with his head down. The kid was taking this personally. He felt responsible, and maybe he was. Maybe they all were, because when the murders had stopped, so had their investigation. They'd abandoned it while the killer wasn't finished, not even close.

And now Luke was missing.

"Hey," Christian said as he entered Tommy's room. "Anything new?"

"Getting back preliminaries from the techs. They've found some hair and they're expediting DNA on it to see if it crosses with anyone already in the system."

"How long will it take?"

"We should know tomorrow," Tommy said. "What about you? Did you go back to your mansion?"

"No."

"What did the shrink say?"

"A bunch of stuff."

"Descriptive," Tommy said.

"Look, I'm going to do it here. You don't have to pay attention to me, just keep working. If you think something is wrong, I want you to shake me, okay?"

"What exactly would 'something wrong' look like?"

"I don't know."

Tommy shook his head. He had actual work to do. He was poring over the case files from six months ago, and now Christian wanted a damned babysitter. "All right, man, but I'm not going to be paying attention to you."

"That's fine."

Christian slumped in his chair and closed his eyes. His body went completely still, and Tommy felt as strange watching him do it this time as he had the first. He understood a lot about Christian, but not this. Not truly. Whatever the kid saw inside himself was something Tommy would never experience, and given Christian's problems, he'd never be able to truly explain it.

There was a gift in it, though. Tommy couldn't deny that.

He looked back at his computer. The lights in his office were off, just like the rest of the floor. The computer screen provided the room's only illumination.

Tommy had never experienced anything like this. He knew that agents died. It was a part of any job where you tried to stop criminals. However, it was a relatively rare thing. Luke had been missing for sixteen hours so far, and everyone knew the first forty-eight were the most important, thanks to that damn television show.

That left them with only thirty-two hours to find him.

Was he strung up already, being pseudo-crucified like an Ancient Roman criminal?

Tommy closed his eyes and tried to push the thought away, knowing it was cancerous. If he let it spread, it'd fill his whole brain with thoughts of what might be happening to Luke, none of which would help him find his partner.

When he opened his eyes, he went back to work studying everything he could find on the Priest.

———

Christian stood outside the room. The blood still dripped from the name above, and the pool at his feet had grown large. There was no stepping over it this time. No avoiding it.

Blood covered the entire hallway. He stood in it, and because he never wore shoes in his mansion, he felt the warmth against his skin. Despite how long it had been pooling here waiting on his return, it still felt freshly spilled.

Christian swallowed, determined not to throw up. The blood was so voluminous because he'd refused to come back. This was his fault.

He pushed open the door and went inside. The vents above were silent, thank God. The door closed behind him, and Christian saw that the blood dripping from his statue's hands had progressed as well. It covered the floor, and when he picked up his feet to walk, tiny droplets fell from his soles.

This place had changed drastically in six months.

*Of course it has. It didn't sit static while you fell in love with Veronica.*

The walls in most rooms were digital, allowing him to pull things up and manipulate data or maps. He could usually read entire case files by simply telling the walls to display them. Not in here.

Large murals surrounded him, showing painful

tortures. He saw the iron maiden, ready to close on a woman, her face a twisted view of terror. Knowing that when it closed, her life on this planet ended.

He saw a person being stretched across the rack, mechanical wheels pulling his body apart.

The torture went on and on across the walls.

Yet, his statue still stood in the center of the room. Blood didn't just drip from his hands and eyes now. It poured out of his eyes, down his face, over his lips, and along his neck. It kept falling until it met the floor's red tide.

The voice came from above. "You're back."

Christian didn't answer. He studied the word patterns and cadence.

He turned to the wall, and where a digital readout should have shown the intricacies of this *other's* words, Christian instead saw a man's entrails being ripped from his stomach.

*So, I'm not in control,* he thought, feeling relatively calm compared to the last time he'd been here.

He turned from the statues and exited the room. He moved down the hall, the blood splashing against the bottom of the walls as he walked. He found Luke's room and turned the knob.

It didn't budge.

He pushed on the door with his shoulder, but nothing happened.

"What is going on?"

"Why do you want to go in there," the voice asked from above.

"What are you?" Christian stared at the unmoving door

as he spoke, but.

"I'm you. Or what you're becoming."

"You sound nothing like me."

"You won't resemble much of your current self when this is done," it said.

"When *what* is done? The Priest?"

The voice laughed, sending a chill across Christian's entire body. His feet were the only part of him that didn't grow cold, warmed by the surrounding blood.

"This didn't begin with the Priest, and it certainly won't end with him, either," the voice said as its laughter subsided. "This is your transformation. When it's over, you won't recognize this place. Or rather, the old you won't. The new version will love it."

"I need to find Luke," Christian said. "I need this place to work until I do, and after that, you can have it. You can do whatever you want with it. But I have to find him."

"You'll find him. I promise."

Christian went back to the Priest's room once more. The door was already open for him.

*It wants me in here,* he thought.

"Yes," the voice said. "*It* does."

Christian walked to the statues and stepped between two kneeling women. He stood directly in front of himself and looked at the bleeding eyes. "So that's what I'll become, someone bathing in blood?"

"Aren't you already? You try to wash it off with Veronica Lopez and your partners, but didn't you start bathing in it the moment you became a field agent? Bradley Brown's dead, but that doesn't mean your guilt vanishes. The people he killed, the responsibility lies as much on you as anyone else."

Christian shook his head. "Then that is on all of us. Tommy and Luke, too."

"Yes. You get it now."

"No one else in the world would say that. Our entire society is built on the premise that each of us controls our own actions."

"What about the Priest?" the voice asked. "Is he controlling his actions? Or is he driven by something else? Look around you. Look at the walls. Were the people that performed those acts under their own control, or did something else drive them?"

*It sounds like Luke,* Christian thought. *He's the only person who could make thoughts like these sound rational.*

"Maybe there's more of Luke in you than you realize."

The voice fell quiet.

Christian turned, looking for another door that might lead to a room where the video would play—the one that would give him insight into the killer.

"There isn't another door, Christian. There is no video to watch. How much time have you spent around the crime scenes? How long did you stare at Ryan Goleen's murder video? How many minutes did you give Mrs. Brown's decapitated head? You've avoided this, and your great mind can't do anything for you, or Luke."

---

Christian's movement pulled Tommy's attention from his computer. He wasn't getting anything from the files anyway. Sometimes detectives and agents missed things the first go-around, but the mind kept working even when the consciousness had moved to something else. Sometimes, when Tommy went back, he saw something new.

Not this time, though.

"Are you okay?"

Christian blinked slowly before straightening up in his chair.

"No. My mind is like a computer file that's got a virus in it."

Tommy shook his head, unable to smile as he normally might when Christian said such ludicrous things. There weren't any smiles inside Tommy right now.

"So, basically, we're right where we started."

"We need to watch the Goleen murder," Christian said as if Tommy hadn't already seen it. "You have the video on your computer?"

"I've watched it ten times, Christian. Others have scoured it. There's nothing to see. The room is nondescript, all you can tell is that it's some kind of storage unit. Even the instruments used, ropes and pulleys, they can be bought anywhere."

"*I* need to watch it again. If you don't want to, fine, but I don't have it on my computer."

Tommy was quiet for a moment. He knew Christian's modus operandi. He nearly had a fetish for being around crime scenes. If Tommy didn't know him, he'd think the kid got off on it. However, Christian remained near them so long, and with so much interest, because it allowed his mind to do what others couldn't.

Yet, he hadn't watched the video more than once?

"Why?"

"Why what?" Christian said.

"Why haven't you watched it more?"

"Because I didn't want to."

"That's not enough," Tommy said. "You're here because of your abilities. If you're blatantly not using them, that's a dereliction of duty. Why didn't you watch it?"

"*Because I killed him!*" Christian shouted. "*He died because of me, just like Bradley's mom!*"

Tears rested in the kid's eyes. After about a minute, filled with silence while Christian wiped his face, Tommy said, "Okay. Pull your chair over here and let's watch it."

It took a few seconds for Tommy to pull up the video and play it. He kept it moving at five times the original pace, speeding through the time where the man hung alone.

"Slow it down."

They both watched the killer crack Goleen's kneecaps. His screams filled the metal room, as well as Tommy's office.

Tommy sped it up again.

"Now. Stop."

Tommy went to normal speed and they watched Ryan Goleen emit his last gasp, a short sucking of air as he tried to pull himself upward using his dislocated shoulders. Then his head sagged against his chest. His eyes were still open, staring down at a floor that he no longer saw.

"Send me the file."

"Okay," Tommy whispered.

"I'll see you in the morning," Christian said.

"You going home?"

"Yes."

With that, Christian got up from the chair and left the building. Tommy looked back at his computer screen and where Ryan Goleen was still hanging, his torture finally finished.

---

Christian went straight home. He speedily tipped his Uber driver as he jumped out of the car before rushing inside.

He lay down on his bed at two in the morning with his laptop propped on his stomach and watched the video again. He did it at twice the speed, a bit slower than the pace Tommy had set.

He went through the video five times before the sun came up. His phone rang an hour later as he was putting his clothes on for work.

*Carla?* he thought. He had her number programmed, although he didn't need it. He had known Carla since he was a child. She was his mother's best friend. Christian had no idea why she'd be calling *him*.

"Hello?"

"Hello, Christian. It's Carla. I'm at your mother's house, but no one is answering. We were supposed to go on our morning walk, but I don't think anyone's home."

"Is her car there?"

"Yes. It's in the driveway. Did she tell you she was going somewhere recently?"

*No. No. No. No.*

Christian hung up the phone and pulled up Tommy's number.

"Hel—"

"No time," Christian said. "Get a pen and paper. Now."
He listened as Tommy rustled for the instruments.

"Okay."

"2987 DePalm Lane. That's my mother's address."

"I know—"

"Get there now and bring whoever the hell you can. You're still at the office, right?"

"Yeah."

"Then you're closer. Get there. I'm on my way."

"What's going on?" Tommy asked.

"The Priest has her."

# CHAPTER SEVENTEEN

Tommy pulled up to the house a few minutes before the local police arrived. The next-door neighbor, an elderly woman with red hair, was walking across her lawn heading for Tommy the moment he exited his car.

"Hi, my name is Carla Britherson. I'm the one who called Christian."

"Ms. Britherson," Tommy said, barely slowing down as he made his way up the driveway, "I need you to go back into your house right now. This may be a crime scene, and it's not safe for you to be here."

"Oh my God," the woman whispered. She stopped walking but didn't turn around. Tommy kept going, not bothering to ensure she left. The police could deal with it.

He went to the front door and banged on it.

"Mrs. Windsor, this is Special Agent Tommy Phillips. Your son sent me over. I need you to open the door right now."

The house spoke with a crypt's voice.

What Tommy needed to do would be a felony if Mrs.

Windsor pressed charges. Christian better make sure she didn't if this all turned out to be bullshit.

He took a step back and kicked just above the door-knob. The wood splintered, then shattered. The door banged open, slamming against the opposite wall.

"Hey!" someone shouted behind him. He didn't know if it was the neighbor or the police, and he didn't care. He unholstered his weapon and moved through the house, clearing it room by room.

No one was here. There was no blood that he could see. No sign of a struggle. Just an empty house without a single light turned on, and the sun shining through the windows.

He heard police moving in through the front door.

"Hello?"

Tommy walked from the back bedroom, pulling out his cellphone. "Put out an APB for Patricia Windsor," he said to one of the officers, passing by and stepping outside onto the yard.

Christian answered the phone on the second ring. "Is she there?"

"No. No one's here. There's been no struggle. I started an APB. Where are you?"

"This goddamn Uber driver is *fucking refusing to speed*!" Christian screamed into the phone. A few seconds passed as the kid regained some composure. "Should be two minutes."

"All right. I'll be here."

The phone went dead and Tommy turned to go back into the house. This could all be for nothing. The woman might have simply had a date and stayed over.

Christian surely wouldn't want to consider that. Yet, it

didn't feel right to Tommy. Maybe Christian's panic was influencing his thinking. Christian's relationship with his mother was borderline unhealthy. She was his most powerful connection to the world. If he even *thought* she was in danger, he'd lose it.

*It's your job to keep him sane, then*, Tommy thought.

He heard a car door open behind him. Christian was jumping out of the Uber before it even came to a complete stop. He rushed by Tommy at a full sprint and went inside the house.

Tommy jogged to catch up, but by the time he reached the living room, Christian was already there, having moved through the entire house.

"He took her."

"You don't know that," Tommy said. "Calm down."

Christian closed his eyes. "There's only one other person. Veronica. Get people at her house now."

———

Veronica answered the door after looking through the peephole.

Two uniformed officers stood on her stoop. Police, not FBI.

"Ms. Lopez? We're with the Atlanta Police Department. May we come in?"

"Sure," Veronica nodded and opened the door wider.

Christian had called her thirty minutes earlier in an absolute panic. She wasn't able to get much from him until Tommy took the phone.

Now the police were here, and Christian was on his

way. She understood what everyone thought was happening, and it took all her willpower to keep from curling into a ball and crying. Her mind kept going back to Bradley Brown and being locked up in that bedroom for what felt like forever.

"I'm Officer Daniels, and this is Officer Krim," the policeman said. "We need to check the house is secure."

"Okay." Veronica paused, and not sure what to say next, she added, "Can I get either of you something to drink?"

"No, ma'am. We're fine. Can you talk with me while Officer Krim secures the house?"

Veronica led Daniels to the living room. Daniels was just about to speak when the front door burst open. Veronica had never seen someone move so quickly. Daniels' weapon was unholstered and pointing at the foyer before she had a chance to move.

"Veronica?" Christian called as he rounded the corner.

"Hey! It's Christian! Put the gun down!"

The cop didn't lower his weapon. He didn't even glance at Veronica. "Keep your hands where I can see them, sir. I need to see your identification."

Tommy came around the corner next, and the cop moved his gun to cover them both as he assessed the new threat.

"I'm Special Agent Phillips. This is Agent Windsor. Here's my ID." He already had it out and his arm extended. The cop approached slowly.

"Okay," he said as he read it. He lowered his weapon. "Sorry. I need to see yours too, sir."

Christian fumbled with his wallet for a second, but

finally retrieved it. He tossed the entire thing to the cop and then walked by him, straight to Veronica.

"Are you okay?" he asked.

"Yes, I'm fine." Her heart was pounding, but the adrenaline spike was lowering some, sending tingles down her arms.

"Thank God."

Christian grabbed her and pulled her close, the most intense form of affection he'd ever shown of his own volition.

She wrapped herself around him, feeling the pressure his arms put on her back.

"What's going on?" Her eyes caught Tommy's, knowing that Christian might not be able to communicate right now.

"We're not completely sure," Tommy said. "His mother isn't at home, but there doesn't appear to have been a struggle. This is all just a precaution."

Veronica nodded and gently forced Christian to take a step back. "Are *you* okay?"

Tears were in his eyes. No answer was needed.

"The house is secure," Officer Krim said as he came in from the back hall. "You two are with the FBI?"

"Yes," Tommy said. "Thank you for getting here so quickly."

"No problem."

The five stood in silence for a moment, until Veronica finally said, "So what's next?"

Lucy stood on the other side of the road from Veronica Lopez's house. She was next to a neighbor's home, her arms twitching at her sides. A massive tree hid her. She'd been standing by it for the past hour. She had watched the police cruiser pull up, and then Christian arrive and run inside.

It nearly broke her heart to see such fear in him.

*He doesn't understand yet. He will, though. There's no need for him to fear anything ever again.*

The demon had told her this would happen. That if she went for Veronica Lopez now, she'd end up getting caught, because the FBI would soon notice Mrs. Windsor was missing. Lucy hadn't believed him, knowing the snake spoke lies as easily as it hissed. So she came and stood by this tree just around the corner of the house so that if anyone walked outside, they wouldn't see her.

Lucy had been patient, intent on watching until her shift at work started. Her hair blew slightly in the wind. She reached up to move it from her face.

So, the demon had been right. Lopez would be watched now.

Lucy needed to pray. She needed to get away from all of this and seek God's wisdom. She couldn't make the right choice about what to do next, not until God spoke. She *knew* the Lord wanted to turn Christian into His vessel, but with all of this happening, she didn't know *how* to do it.

*If the Lord is for me, who can be against me?* she thought, but it didn't hold its usual power.

Lucy hadn't listened to Luke regarding Mrs. Windsor, and that was unfortunate. The Priestess took Christian's mother back to wherever she lived, which could create problems if the woman wasn't careful. The transportation of kidnap victims was a dangerous enterprise.

The Priestess could not be caught until Luke was finished.

The light above never went off and Luke remained directly beneath it. He was alone with his thoughts.

There were a lot of possibilities in the air, and he wasn't sure the Priestess was up to the challenge. With Bradley Brown, Luke had engineered everything. Now, he could only *influence* things, and only when the woman returned.

He needed contact with Windsor's mother. That, and for Ms. Lopez to show up. Luke thought Christian was already changing. He had to be, given the events taking place. All of which were necessary, if not sufficient, for Christian's eventual rebirth.

Luke was in this for the long game, obviously, or else Christian would already be dead. However, the game had now started in earnest.

Lucy did her best to ignore the woman in the back bedroom. It wasn't that hard, because Mrs. Windsor kept quiet, yet Lucy still wanted to speak with her. There were so many things she could learn from the woman, things about Christian that only a mother would know.

Now wasn't the time. She needed to seek God's guidance, not rely on worldly messages. Listening to that demon sitting in the storage unit had gotten her in a whole heap of trouble, and she knew God was already displeased. Daddy had taught her that God was merciful but also vengeful.

Perhaps this confusion rising inside her was His vengeance.

Lucy double-checked the apartment door's deadbolt and then turned to her living room. It didn't look the way she wanted yet, but she hadn't lived here long.

A large picture of Christ on the cross hung from the wall in the spot where most people would have a television. The single piece of furniture, an old rocking chair she'd bought for five bucks, sat in the middle of the room, facing Christ.

Daddy had taught her that while many people might have happy pictures of Jesus, him feeding children or tending a flock, those people were not true Christians. Jesus suffered, and He did it for the sins of people. Those people should remember that suffering.

The painting was intricate in its detail. Lucy sat in the chair and stared at the twisted face full of pain and mourning. She looked at the blood running down His forehead, over His eyebrows, and into His eyes; all stemming from the mocking crown that sat atop His head. King of the Jews. It sickened her and made her feel rage at those Romans long since dead.

"Forgive them father, for they know not what they do," she mumbled, her lip twitching as she prayed.

The prayer helped calm her.

She hadn't done the ritual her father taught her in a

long time, not for at least two years. The ritual, or lack of it, was perhaps why God no longer spoke to her.

Lucy stood and went to the kitchen. She reached under the sink and pulled out a rope, a thick one she'd gotten from the Home Depot when she first left Greenbriar. She hadn't used it because she didn't want to. It scared her. Always had. Her daddy was the one who said it was necessary, and she supposed it was. She still held a deep fear of it. Before pulling it out, she looked at the whip she'd bought, knowing that it might come to *that*…

But not yet. Maybe this would be enough.

She brought the rope to the living room and tied a loop over the front door's knob. This wasn't how her daddy did it. He had been more prepared than she was. But it would work.

She tied the noose quickly with sure movements that came from years of practice. She knelt down in front of the door and slipped the loop over her head, where it fell home around her neck.

Lucy knelt and leaned forward, feeling the rough rope tighten across her skin. She kept leaning and God's instrument grew tight. She went forward further still, and her vision began graying, the edges turning dark and the room in front of her growing hazy.

Finally, Lucy collapsed on her side, darkness taking over.

God spoke to her then, just like her father had taught her He would.

# CHAPTER EIGHTEEN

"The hair has no match. If he was arrested, it had to be with local cops somewhere. Nothing federal, and nothing to get a DNA sample from it," Agent Bench said.

Tommy nodded, already having figured as much. Tommy, Christian, and Perry Bench were sitting at the small conference table in Tommy's office. The speaker-phone was in the middle of the table, with Waverly listening.

"We haven't heard from Windsor's mother?" the Director asked.

Tommy looked at Christian, who was staring blankly at the speakerphone. Tommy wasn't sure he actually saw it.

"No, sir," Tommy said

"How sure are we that her going missing is related to the Priest?"

"It's been twenty-four hours, sir. The killer took Luke, then, we believe, Mrs. Windsor. Our best theory is that this is some sort of religious ritual built around Windsor."

"Do we have any evidence to support this outside of the Goleen video?" Waverly asked.

"The cross on the decapitated head, but other than that, no."

"Okay, let's go with this for now, but I don't want any of you singularly focused on that theory."

They'd spent the past fifteen hours discussing possible theories, as well as sending out directives to field agents. Tommy was completely confident with what he was about to say, and Christian was also on board. Bench, for the most part, concerned himself with the operational aspects instead of strategy. Tommy had to throw this at the wall and see if it stuck. Waverly was the wall.

"Yes, sir. The research we completed last night points toward a backwoods version of Christianity that is still sometimes practiced in the deep south. It's been dying off quickly in the past decade. There is a similarity to the strand of Catholicism, Opus Dei, but only in the ritualistic abuse that people put themselves through. Da Vinci Code type stuff. The backwoods version we're talking about focuses on Jesus Christ's suffering—"

"Hold on, Phillips," Waverley cut in. "What makes you think that's what we're dealing with here? Some redneck sect of Christianity?"

"The way Ryan Goleen was killed," Christian said, his voice ice that'd been frozen in the arctic tundra for a thousand years. "There's a history of crucifixion in these sects. Often they crucify animals as a ritual sacrifice, but within the past fifty years there have been records of at least two incidents from South Florida where people were crucified."

"That's a weak connection, guys. Goleen was strung up, not put on a cross."

"But his body formed a cross," Christian said, and Tommy noticed he didn't use the word "sir." "The cross on Mrs. Brown's face is another piece of evidence as well."

"All right. Let's say you're right," Waverly said. "What does any of this have to do with you?"

Christian's mouth remained closed, so Tommy continued. "These sects believe God speaks directly to them during some of the ritualistic abuse they perform on themselves. God is an active part of their lives, active in the sense that while they can read the Bible, they can just as easily talk directly to Him if they perform the rituals regularly. Now, these sects are different as there's no formal organization, but most believe that God will send someone to cleanse the world before Jesus returns. The Second Coming will be more of a glorification than a reckoning. Jesus won't dirty his hands with it, because the one before Him will have killed off the wicked."

"So this psycho believes Windsor is basically Jesus reborn?"

"Not, exactly, but close. He's the one that will make the way for Jesus," Tommy said.

"So why is he killing people?"

"Sacrifices to Windsor. When they harm themselves, they're giving sacrifice of their body to Jesus, and the same with animals. We think this is his way of letting Windsor know 'God's plan.'"

"Why did he take Christian's mother, then?" Waverly asked.

"We're not sure, sir. If our theory is correct, then harming the savior's mother wouldn't make sense."

"No, it wouldn't."

Silence fell across the room.

"Okay. Look, I don't really buy all that. It's too fucking flimsy, but it doesn't really matter. Tell me what your plan is."

If the theory was bad, the plan might even be worse. The plan wasn't exactly nonexistent, but they were working off of basically nothing. Bench helped create it. Christian had been silent for the most part. He only seemed concerned with getting back to Veronica's house, although her place was under twenty-four-hour surveillance. It was like the kid knew he couldn't save his mother or Luke, so all that mattered was keeping someone else from being abducted.

"We still have agents scouring through storage companies, though getting warrants for the companies that won't let us in is a growing problem. We're focusing on storage units in the Atlanta area since we don't think our guy is transporting people over long distances. We are going back to the care facility where Mrs. Brown resided, checking to see if there were any unusual visitors preceding her abduction and murder. They've been blocking us, so we may need a warrant there as well. We're tracking all of Luke's credit card purchases, as well as Mrs. Windsor's, in case the killer needs cash. We've got twenty-four-hour surveillance on both my girlfriend and Christian's. Today we're going through Christian's history to understand if there is anyone who might have harmed him in the past, and we'll be sending protection to them as well. Many of his professors are already being watched, though we haven't alerted them—"

"So basically," Waverly interjected, "we're waiting on this guy to strike again."

"Yes, sir."

Another long pause, and when Waverly spoke, emotion filled the room. "Look, Luke is one of ours, and this son-of-a-bitch has Christian's mother. I don't need to tell you what the hell I'm thinking because you're thinking it too. Don't let either of them get harmed. Christian, you there?"

"Yes."

"When we get off the phone, I want you to call me back privately, okay?"

"Okay." Christian didn't so much as nod.

"I don't want anyone knowing what we're doing. The press doesn't know about Luke or Mrs. Windsor. Keep it that way. I want this motherfucker thinking he's safe and can take whoever he wants. Use local police, hell, local militias if they have any down there. Just make sure everyone that could be a target is watched constantly."

"Yes, sir," Tommy said.

"Call me, Christian."

The line went dead and Tommy looked at his partner. He didn't glance up from the speaker.

"You better go call him." Tommy turned to Bench. "New reports came in thirty minutes ago. You need to use the bathroom or anything? Or you ready to look through them?"

"Let's get started," Bench said.

Christian stood and silently left the room.

"It's me," Christian said into his cellphone.

"How are you holding up?" the Director asked.

Christian stood in the FBI's parking lot. It was six in the morning and cars were pulling in. He stood in between two parked vehicles so that he'd have semi-privacy while he spoke. Christian could have gone to his office for more privacy, but he couldn't stand being between walls anymore. It made him think of the four walls Goleen had stared at while dying. The four walls his mother might be staring at right now.

"I'm fine."

"I know you're not, but I didn't have you call me to discuss it. I talked to Phillips, and he said you're holding back on this," Waverly said. "I know what you did with Brown two years ago, though it hasn't been widely publicized inside the FBI. I know about the connections your mind makes. Phillips hasn't told me a lot, but he's told me enough."

Christian said nothing as the Director paused. He didn't feel anger at Tommy for telling Waverly. Tommy would do his job regardless of what happened, and that meant alerting Waverly to Christian's mental state.

"This is an order, so I don't want you to think that I'm trying to assuage your feelings right now. Whatever is holding you back, or keeping you from making the connections that you usually do, I'm telling you to kill it right now. If you hold back on this and anyone else dies, you're out of the FBI. I don't know if that matters to you anymore, but that's where we are. If you give it your all and we still fail, fine, but I'm not going to have you putting people at risk because of some mental block you refuse to face."

Christian swallowed. Hate fueled him. Hate for the man on the phone talking as if Christian didn't care about his mother or partner. Hate for the person who took them. Hate for himself for being so weak.

"Do you hear me?" Waverly barked.

"Yes."

"Good. You three call me tonight by six, and that's at the latest."

The line went dead and Christian slowly lowered the phone from his ear. He stood in the parking lot, people walking inside the building behind him. No one looked at him. Most were staring at their phones or listening to the music pumping through their headphones.

Christian was finding it hard to focus. He couldn't stop thinking about his mother, Veronica, or Luke. He was filled with emotions he barely understood. He didn't have time for Melissa, didn't even have time to talk to *Veronica*. There was work to do.

Everyone around him was screaming at him to go to his mansion, and even though he'd returned once, that had been the last time.

It had to end, though. The Director was right. The emotions filling him now would be nothing compared to what he'd feel if...

*She's already dead. He is, too. You know that. Going back into your mansion may help you catch the killer, but it's not going to save them.*

Christian closed his eyes.

It was true. It had to be. Two days had passed since Luke's disappearance and another since his mother's. The killer wasn't keeping them in limbo. It wouldn't fit with his past crimes. He abducted and then he killed.

*Stop it,* his mother said.

Christian opened his eyes and saw her standing directly in front of him. He didn't avert his gaze like usual. He didn't care if people saw him talking to someone who wasn't there. He looked directly at the image his brain projected, his mom in the flesh.

*I might be dead or I might not be. If I am, then we had a great time together, and if I'm not, you sitting out here whining won't help anyone. You've done more in your life than anyone I've ever met, and you've done it with a whole host of issues that other people can't imagine. This is the most important thing that's ever been put in front of you, and you better not cower from it, son.*

Christian reached up to wipe the tears from his eyes. When he put his hands down, his mother was gone, and only the parking lot lay in front of him.

"Okay," he said. "Okay."

He turned around and walked back into the office.

---

A smile bloomed inside Luke, though his face remained motionless.

Mrs. Windsor lay before him, a dark pillowcase over her face. Her hands and legs were bound, most likely there was tape or something else over her mouth preventing her from speaking since she was silent.

The Priestess stood in front of Luke, a little smirk on her face.

"You brought her," Luke said. "Did you finally see it was too risky keeping her at your place?"

"There is no risk for me in any of this. I brought her because the Lord told me to. He said it's okay if she gets to know you better so that when you die, she'll see the truth about her son."

Luke knew he should stay quiet, but he couldn't help himself. Pain could come at any moment from this woman, but prodding her—or anyone with such a mental state— brought him a bit of joy.

"Did the Lord tell you to keep Christian's mother gagged and tied up?"

Her right eyebrow twitched, giving her a humorous look. "It's necessary right now. She'll be freed soon enough, unlike you, serpent."

"Did God talk to you about Veronica Lopez? Did you go see her? Is she being watched, like I said?"

Luke needed to be careful. Mrs. Windsor was hearing everything and to give away too much could cause horrible problems later. Luke could fix them by simply killing Christian's mother, but he didn't want that just yet.

"What God says to me isn't for you to hear, swine."

Which meant yes. Luke's plan was working, and Veronica Lopez would be brought here. He just had to hope that Christian was kept away long enough for her arrival. That was the missing variable that Luke no longer controlled. He set things in motion, of course, but Christian's mind was special, as was his personality. Luke could plan and predict, but the power that rested in Christian's head couldn't be fully controlled.

"Well, I hope you hurry with whatever God told you. I'm sure the FBI is getting closer by the second."

The woman glared at him for a moment, her face doing its little dance. Luke smiled and then watched as her hand closed into a fist and pain exploded across his face. She hit him directly in his already swollen eye. Blackness threatened to swarm, but Luke focused and pushed it back. He concentrated on his breath as the stars in front of him faded, and he found himself looking at the Priestess again.

She smiled now.

Luke remained still.

Her death would hurt worse than she could imagine. He wondered if her God knew that.

The woman went to Mrs. Windsor and took the bag off her face. She pulled the tape from her mouth in one quick motion, and to Mrs. Windsor's credit, she didn't say anything, although the pain she felt was written across her face.

Finally, the Priestess left without saying anything else. Luke heard the padlock click in place.

He looked at Christian's mother, and despite the pain he felt, he offered her a sad smile.

Time to go to work.

# CHAPTER NINETEEN

Christian spent the day with Tommy and Bench. They went through Christian's entire history, outlining everyone that could be a possible target. Plans were set in motion to watch them, most without the potential targets being aware of their new protection. The key to Tommy's plan was ensuring that everything looked exactly as it should. Nothing out of the ordinary, so they could lure the killer out.

Christian finally left the office at eleven that night. He called Veronica on the way home, ensuring that she was okay. She said the car was still outside her house and hadn't left her the entire time. The two cops had even sat on her floor at work.

"They follow me to the bathroom. Or at least, the bathroom is visible when I'm in it. It's lovely."

Christian didn't smile at the joke.

He wanted to go to her house and sleep there, which for him was something akin to lighting himself on fire. He couldn't, though. Not tonight. He was going somewhere else, and for once, going inside *that* place was more terrifying than spending time with the people outside of it.

Christian made it home and went to his bed, laying down and taking a deep breath. He closed his eyes.

He started in the mansion's foyer. He looked up the staircase and saw trails of blood beginning to leak all the way down here. It wasn't an inch thick on the floor like in other areas. It hadn't even reached where he was standing, but it would soon without a doubt.

He pushed the thought away.

He walked past the stairs and turned right. Something might be in here with him, but it didn't fully control the place yet. Christian still held some sway, and he felt his mansion expanding as he moved through it. An entire hallway was constructed as he approached it. He didn't know how long he could keep control over the mansion, nor how deep the voice had permeated the building, but he had some time.

He just needed to use it.

Christian found himself at a large rotunda. The hallway dead-ended into it. The rotunda was shoddily constructed from stone, but the necessary pieces were there. He couldn't enter or control the Priest's room, but at least for now, he could use this.

A television sat in front of him, and a chair in front of that. The chair was made from the same stone as the rotunda, nothing like the comfortable furniture he usually sat in while watching the horrors take place.

He sat and the television clicked on.

Christian looked above him and saw no vents. He heard no whispers at all.

*Go*, he thought.

---

The first thing Christian sees is that the Priest is no priest. He is, in fact, not a *he* at all. The Priest is a *she*.

Christian's eyes widen as he stares at the teenage girl. Her face is still clouded. The girl is standing in an old church. The pews are all wooden without any cushions on them. There are only five. The girl is in the main aisle, and she holds a book pressed against her chest.

Christian walks closer and sees that it's a Bible.

The girl is crying.

"Why?" Christian says.

The girl, of course, doesn't look at him. She doesn't hear him at all.

She is staring at the large wooden cross on the pulpit. A plastic Jesus rests on it, looking cheap and almost humorous in its attempt to show the savior's suffering. Parts of the cross have been painted red. Christian assumes that's to portray Jesus' blood. The whole thing looks like a Halloween display that charges two dollars for a tour.

The girl breaks her stare and walks outside the church. Christian follows. They go to a field in the back where there's a hole in the ground with four people standing around it. One of them is the preacher, who stands at the head of the hole.

He's a fat, unshaven man, and he's sweating profusely underneath the afternoon sun. Sweat stains have spread through his short sleeve, button-up shirt. It was white this morning, but now his perspiration shows large swaths of his skin through the shirt.

"And the Lord said, we'll all turn into dust again,"

"Again" sounds like "ehgin" to Christian.

Christian ignores the preacher and watches the girl. She walks up to an older man, perhaps in his forties. Christian sees the disapproving look the man gives her. He says nothing, and the girl keeps her eyes on the ground. She clutches the Bible to her chest as if it were a shield.

The preacher finishes speaking and the older man looks down at the girl. "Go on. Give it to your mother."

The girl moves to the grave and kneels. Christian has to walk closer to see as she reaches in and lays the Bible down.

There is no coffin inside. Only the body of a woman wearing a purple dress. The face is bruised and battered. Purple skin and split cheeks, showing the bone beneath. The throat is still swollen with large blue veins trying to burst from it.

The girl stares for a moment longer and then scurries back.

Christian keeps on looking until everyone leaves and the world around him goes black.

---

Christian blinked as the video ended.

"What is this?" the voice asked. "A new room? One hastily created, clearly."

Christian looked above him and saw a vent that hadn't been there when he first started watching the film.

"My question is, Christian: Why do you want to catch her? You do realize what you could be right? A god, right here on Earth. That girl would die for you. She would, and has, killed for you. She'll continue to. Why don't you want that?"

Christian sighed but said nothing. He looked at the television in front of him, wishing it would go on. Wishing he could know what happened to the woman in the dirt, and why.

"I'll leave you be. You can keep watching. Just think about it. Why catch her? Why not train her instead?"

The television turned back on and Christian went forth.

---

"What I'm about to do…it's essential."

The man stands on his porch, his daughter next to him. They are the same people from the funeral. Christian is four feet to the man's right.

"And you're going to have to watch it."

The girl's eyes are wide and fat tears stream down her face. They seem to come from an endless supply. The wooden porch beneath her is wet with them, yet they continue falling.

"Duh-duh-Daddy," the girl says, but she doesn't finish the sentence.

"Hush," the father says. "I don't want to hear nothin' from you about this. God already spoke to me."

Christian takes a step behind the father and looks at his back. The man is wearing a white t-shirt, but it does little to hide his wounds. Large stripes of blood cross the shirt like rivers. Christian doesn't know what the rest of his body looks like beneath his clothing, but there appears to be long gashes all over him.

"If she won't believe, then God ain't never gonna talk to us," the man says. He's not looking at his daughter.

He is still staring out across the front yard when the girl falls down, collapsing right on the porch. The tears still flee her eyes and she begins to whine, a sound that threatens to make Christian's ears bleed.

The father finally breaks his concentration and looks at his daughter. "Stop it."

The girl doesn't stop. The whine continues until the man reaches down and picks her up, slinging her over his shoulder. Christian can't imagine the pain that must accost the man with the added weight on his back, but the father only gives a slight grimace.

He walks into the house and Christian follows. He doesn't look at the area around him as he tries to keep up. The man is walking quickly.

They move straight through the house and into the backyard. There's a shed in the back and Christian has no doubt that's where the man is heading.

The three of them cross the yard. Christian looks around and sees there are no other houses anywhere. They are alone, with only tall grass fields and the insects they hold for company.

The man reaches the shed and opens it. There is no lock. No need for security in a place this remote.

Christian follows the two inside. A dingy overhead light bulb is the only light in this place. It casts a yellow glow across everything, making the room look diseased.

A woman lies on the ground, and that's exactly what it is, just dirt ground. Her arms and legs are tied with tight knots. She is the same woman from the funeral. Her face is already beat to shit, and her eyes are so swollen that there's no way she can see.

She breathes into the dirt and particles fly up around her face, landing and sticking to her bloodied skin. She says nothing.

*Is it because she knows it won't matter?*

The man drops the girl to the ground. She's still making that awful noise. Her thumb is in her mouth and her legs are curled up to her chest as if she's regressed to an infantile state.

"Sit up," the father says.

The girl doesn't move.

"Sit *up!*"

His voice slaps through the room like a whip, and the girl *does* move. She sits up and quickly pushes herself all the way to the wall, leaning her back against it and staring at her mother.

"I tried to make her believe. You've got to understand that. If you don't understand anything else, understand I tried." The man's southern drawl is thick, almost a caricature.

The woman breathes heavily on the dirt floor.

"She ain't never believed, though, and God ain't going to send us what we're waiting on if someone like this is in our midst. The Bible says not to suffer a witch, and a whore is pretty similar to a witch in my eyes. In God's, too. Your mother is a whore, and if it ain't with other men, then it's with other ideas from this sick planet. I won't suffer her in my house any longer."

The girl says nothing, only sucks her thumb and continues crying. The horrible whine has stopped. She's completely silent.

The man kneels down next to his wife and rubs his hand through her hair like a caring lover.

"You should have believed," he says.

Christian sees no tears in his eyes. His voice carries the concern of a man doing a duty, but not one he finds joy in.

He turns the woman on her back and straddles her stomach. Christian can finally see the woman's full face, the yellow light from above painting everything with a jaundiced tint. Her eyes are wide and full of fear, different from her daughter's, which appear almost dead. They don't contain tears, though.

Husband and wife look at each other dry-eyed. and then the man wraps his hands around the woman's throat.

Christian sees the strong cords of muscle bulging beneath his skin and his face twists in a wicked snarl. The woman begins gurgling, her feet kicking up and down behind her husband, doing everything in their power to grant her lungs air. She can't move her arms because the man is sitting on them.

Her head twists left and right and clods of dirt grab onto her hair. She can't escape. Spit flies from her mouth, landing on her lips. The bright white foam reveals the woman's dehydration. Her skin is turning blue.

With Bradley Brown, Christian had wanted to turn away, but now he doesn't. He wants to watch this man kill.

"Yes," a voice says to him.

Christian doesn't turn to his left, where the voice comes from. He can see a shadow standing in his peripheral vision.

"Watch her die. Brutality is necessary in this life, Christian. Necessary, and even right sometimes."

Veins bulge across the woman's forehead, and the strangling continues for five minutes or so. Christian doesn't turn away. He wasn't aware it took so long to strangle someone.

Finally, the life inside the woman is gone, and the man falls over to the side. He lies on his back, his chest heaving.

Minutes pass in silence. The girl still sits against the wall, not moving. She stares straight ahead as if nothing happened.

Finally, her father speaks, although it's difficult for him to catch his breath. "Father Martin says the church will take care of it. All of this is okayed by everyone. It was the only thing we could do."

---

"It's not a pretty life, is it?" the voice said. "The father quoting scripture and discussing why the mother must die. I wonder, will the daughter quote scripture when Luke dies? Did she quote it for Goleen?"

There was more here and Christian knew it, but he didn't want to stay any longer.

The voice that spoke from the vent was starting to sound sweeter. Not something that he wanted to run from, but maybe something he'd like to hear more of.

"Go on, then, Christian. I'll be here when you're ready to learn about our girl."

# CHAPTER TWENTY

While Christian was watching Lucy Speckle's history, Lucy watched Veronica Lopez in reality. Or, rather, she watched the world around Veronica Lopez.

The night was late and the road dark. Streetlights were spaced every thirty feet or so, but Lucy had no problem remaining in the shadows.

She looked at the car sitting across the street from Lopez's house. Two heads were sticking up just above the seats. Lucy had been staring at the car for the past hour, at a distance of fifty feet. Her body did its dance and twitch as usual, and as usual, Lucy didn't notice.

Lucy's thoughts were on the two cops.

The Lord had spoken to her, just as Daddy said He would. The Lord had told her what her daddy had about Momma.

*Don't suffer a witch, and a whore is pretty much the same thing.*

This woman was a whore, and while the demon may have suggested Lucy take her, the Lord was the one who gave the final direction. The demon didn't know it, but he was playing right into God's plan, which made sense to Lucy. Everything served God.

A pistol sat lodged in between her stomach and her pants. She'd taken it from Luke Titan's house. She had shot guns when she was younger, with her daddy, so she wasn't concerned about using them. After throwing Titan in the trunk, she had found a suppressor in Titan's house and had attached it to reduce the noise factor.

Daddy and the church showed her a lot about guns, so while the designs had changed over the years, the basics remained the same. Really, the demon had supplied her with everything she needed to do this job, including the getaway car.

Lucy moved around the back of the house where she was hiding. She crept across the unfenced yard, moving diagonally to the very edge of the property. She crossed two yards like that and had to scale a fence on the second, but that was easy.

Now she stood about a hundred feet in front of the cop car, behind another house. The night was silent. No dogs sensed her presence, and there was no movement from any of the houses.

Lucy pulled her hoodie off her head and started walking. She moved across the lawn and entered the street in front of the two police officers. She wanted to be seen. Her hoodie covered the gun's bulge.

The two police officers simultaneously opened their doors, breaking the night's silence. The cop in the driver's seat shined a flashlight, blinding Lucy a bit. That was okay. She knew where they were standing.

"Ma'am, please stop right there."

Lucy did.

For all the twitches and shakes her body gave, her father had trained her well with a gun. She whipped it from her pants and fired two bullets into the cop on the passenger side, while the other dropped the flashlight and scrambled for his own weapon.

She shot him as he raised it. He collapsed to the ground.

Lucy stood in the silence, the flashlight still shining across the ground. It showed the cop's leg twitching and that made Lucy smile. She didn't know why.

Lucy walked forward and turned the flashlight off, leaving the two bodies in darkness. She didn't bother picking them up. She didn't plan on being inside the house long. She *did* close the doors on each side before walking off. She didn't want the interior lights shining.

She felt confident as she walked across the street. She knew God was with her, and while He may have abandoned her for a bit to teach her a lesson, she was on the right path once more.

---

Veronica woke at a noise that could have been a car backfiring and froze. Completely. She couldn't breathe, her lungs seizing up like an engine without oil. The lights inside her bedroom were off, and she lay in darkness with the covers pulled to her neck.

She strained to hear, and though she had been asleep moments before, the night's sluggishness had been cast off like a groom's pants on his wedding night.

A brittle sound cut through the silence.

*That was glass. That was glass breaking,* her mind said, oddly calm despite her inability to move or breathe.

The kitchen door swung open.

Veronica wanted to say something, to ask who was there. Maybe it was the police, or maybe...maybe it was Christian. That's what her mind tried telling her, but deep down where Veronica's dark thoughts lived, she knew the truth.

She shouldn't have made it out of Bradley Brown's house alive, and every moment since had been time stolen from death. Now death had come to collect what was owed.

*The alarm. The alarm is going off.*

That was true, regardless of anything else happening right now. She had set the alarm before going to bed. The cops were being alerted. Someone would come.

"Get up."

The voice spoke from the bedroom door. It wasn't a man. No way. That was a woman.

"I said get *up!*"

Veronica jumped, moving for the first time since waking. She scooted back against her headboard, keeping the covers pulled up to her neck. She could make out a figure in the darkness. The intruder looked thin. Skinny, even.

"Okay. Have it your way," the woman said.

Veronica watched her move, frozen once more, and a single thought went through her head.

*She's so fast.*

Pain erupted on the side of Veronica's face, followed by

a dark explosion with rings of light outlining it. The rings spread the pain across her head, and darkness followed until it owned everything.

---

Luke watched the woman waking. He'd been staring at her for the past two hours, having decided that when he left this building, he'd paint a picture of Mrs. Windsor lying bound on the floor. He memorized each detail, from the way the light above cast tiny shadows across the thousands of ridges on the concrete floor, to how her hair hung behind her ear as she slept.

Luke closed his eyes and let his head slump down to his chest just before the woman opened her own eyes.

He heard her move and pretended to slowly wake, blinking and looking around the room as if he hadn't seen it for hours.

Luke's eyes found Mrs. Windsor's. She was pulling herself up and trying to push her body back against the wall so she could sit.

"Have you been awake long?" he said. "I don't know when I dozed off."

"No. I just woke up. She hasn't been back, I take it?" Mrs. Windsor said.

"I don't think so."

The woman sighed and Luke turned his gaze to the metal door.

"No sense in screaming, is there?" she said.

"I don't think so. I tried earlier, but I don't think a lot of sound escapes."

A pause followed, and then Mrs. Windsor asked, "Do you know why she's doing this?"

"The obvious answer is she's insane, but I don't think that's what you're wanting," Luke said.

"Yeah, I'd like a little more substance."

Luke looked back to her, his face showing a warmth that had been absent the past two hours. A look that portrayed one message: they were in this together.

"I'm not totally sure, but I believe she thinks your son is either Christ, or a harbinger of him, and through sacrificing people, Christian will realize this—ooof." Luke stopped, grimacing. It was, of course, faked, but he needed to humanize himself for this woman. "Sorry. She really did a number on my head. She believes that by sacrificing people, Christian will realize his fate. She honestly believes she's saving the world."

"So she's going to sacrifice us?"

"No. She's going to kill me, and probably the next person she brings here. I think you're just going to be made to watch us die."

"Oh, that sounds pleasant," Mrs. Windsor said, laughing without humor and shaking her head. "Do you have any kind of plan to get out of this?"

Luke blinked and looked forward at the door. "No," he said, not lying to the woman. "I've got no idea how to free us."

"Don't worry, I've got no plans either."

Luke liked her humor. "At least you can laugh in a situation like this."

"It's either that or cry." Mrs. Windsor paused. "Do you think Christian will find us? Or Tommy?"

"I know that they're both doing everything they can. I think if we could convince her to bring Christian here, that would easily solve this."

"Bring him here? Into this? He won't be able to handle it. I mean, I know how awful this will sound, but she could kill *him*, too."

Luke nodded. "I think he can handle it. He's a remarkable person, Mrs. Windsor, and if he comes here, I'm betting Tommy and a host of other agents will, too."

A few minutes passed in silence, and then Mrs. Windsor said, "I appreciate you saving my son. It feels weird to say that, but I do."

Luke smiled. "Let's hope he returns the favor."

A car door shut outside, hard. He hated that the bitch was driving his Tesla around. Out of everything she'd done, perhaps that was the most unforgivable. Luke had, indeed, provoked his brief beating. But her to be driving his vehicle around with bodies in the trunk nearly made him vomit.

"She's here," Mrs. Windsor said, pulling her knees to her chest, though she couldn't wrap her arms around them due to her constraints.

"It's okay. Just stay calm. Listen to me, now," Luke said, still looking at the door. "It's important you pretend to buy into what she believes. You *know* your son *is* what she says, and you've just been basically babysitting for the past three decades. Whatever I say during this time is in hopes of getting us out of here, so you'll need to go along with it. Okay?"

The woman said nothing.

"Okay?"

"Yes, yes. Sure."

"Stay calm," Luke repeated.

The padlock was removed and then Luke watched as the hanging door slid up.

The Priestess tossed Veronica in as if she weighed no more than a bag of lettuce. Luke was curious what the Priestess looked like underneath her clothing. Not in a sexual manner. He imagined her body must resemble a Greek sculpture with dazzling muscle to have such strength.

"The whore and the Devil." She turned around and shut the door. The metal clanged against the concrete and the sound echoed off the walls. She looked at Luke. "Now, we can begin."

"I'm curious how you plan on getting your message out to Christian?" Luke said. "I'm just not sure how well thought out all of this is. Did you come up with the idea, or was it God?"

"It's nuh-nuh-none of your concern what my plan is, demon." She moved to the back wall and started carrying the cross and tools so that Luke could watch her work. "If you talk any more, I'm guh-guh-going to use your gun to knock your teeth down your throat."

*That's a lot of 'your' in one sentence,* Luke thought. He kept his mouth shut. He didn't want to leave this place needing dental work. A scar or two he could deal with, but to have his teeth replaced was akin to this woman driving his car.

The Priestess got to work and Luke sat in silence, watching. Waiting for what he knew would begin soon. Veronica was still knocked out and Luke had to hope that her brains weren't scrambled from this imbecile's brute strength. For the second time, he'd managed to have a psychopath capture her. She might have thought they moved past her little endeavor in uncovering his past deeds, but the truth was, Luke would see her dead.

"It's an honor to meet you, Muh-muh-muh-muh." The Priestess stopped talking and stopped nailing the wood together. "Meh-meh- *Mrs.* Windsor. M-my name is L-l-luh-lucy."

*Oh, Zeus help us all*, Luke thought. She was going to keep stuttering. Luke didn't need more reasons to hate God, but this was something he couldn't overlook. Out of all the people to put in Luke's path, God picked one with an extremely annoying tic.

"Hi, Lucy," Mrs. Windsor said. "It's an honor to be properly introduced to *you*."

Oh, this was good.

"Wuh-why?" Lucy averted her gaze from Christian's mother.

"Because no one else sees what you do."

The young woman looked up, the light from above illuminating her face and showing the hope in it. How long had it been since this creature felt such a thing—not the false hope of the false god she prayed to, but actual hope from a *human being*?

"That my son is the world's savior. I've been waiting for someone like you to come along."

Luke closed his eyes and, once again, did everything in his power to keep from breaking into a smile. He was having a good time.

# CHAPTER TWENTY-ONE

Tommy placed his cellphone down. He sat up in his bed, the lights off around him.

"Do you have to go?" Alice asked.

Tommy closed his eyes and took in a deep breath. He didn't want to speak, not to Alice nor anyone else. Not with the news he'd just received.

*Alarm was triggered. Police showed up and found two dead officers. Veronica Lopez is missing.*

Tommy had simply ended the call. He could have raged, demanding answers, but it wouldn't matter one bit. The only thing that mattered was the next call he had to make.

"Honey?"

"Yes," he said, his eyes still closed. "I have to leave."

"What's going on?"

"He got Veronica."

"Jesus Christ," Alice whispered.

Tommy stood, then reached back to the bed and grabbed his phone. He walked across the bedroom and out onto the condo's balcony. He looked at the city, seeing Atlanta's night skyline before him.

"How is he doing this?"

The wind answered him, whispering so quietly that it might not have spoken at all.

Tommy dialed Christian and put the phone to his ear.

"Hey," Christian said, his voice sounding excited.

"He got Veronica," Tommy said. "The two cops are dead and she's missing."

Silence came back over the phone, stretching on so long that Tommy finally had to say, "Are you there?"

"He's not a he. He's a she."

The phone line went dead.

---

The Priestess was sitting in front of Christian's mother, her legs folded in what kids used to call Indian Style. Luke wasn't sure if that was considered politically incorrect nowadays. The whims of people were so fickle. While millions died from malaria, social justice warriors fought for equal screen time for male and female co-hosts on network news.

Luke understood God, although not why he insisted on keeping such a primitive species alive and on top of the food chain, at that. Of course, God couldn't actually be classified as a "he" at all, but that was Luke's small protest against the social justice warriors.

"You see why I'm doing this, then?" Lucy's speech impediment had fallen away as her mind became wrapped up in the conversation.

"Yes, of course. I've always known Christian was meant for something great. I'm surprised the media hasn't figured it out yet," Mrs. Windsor said.

Lucy shook her head and stared down at her legs. "They won't get it until *he* finally does, but then it'll be too late. Then they'll have to pay for their wicked ways."

"Bring him here," Mrs. Windsor. "Bring my son and show him what you've done for him."

Luke had been looking straight ahead, acting as if Lucy's threats were keeping him quiet when he really wanted to let the two speak. Now, he turned and looked at Christian's mother. She was following his suggestion.

"Do you think he's ready?" Lucy asked.

"He will be. Once he sees all of this. Once he witnesses what you're going to do to Dr. Titan over there."

Luke watched as Mrs. Windsor flicked her eyes toward him before looking back at Lucy.

"He'll have police around him," the Priestess said. "He'll be on high alert. If they catch me, I'll never get the chance to do this. He has to understand *first*."

"Not true," Luke said, looking back toward the door. "If you let me talk to Christian, I can get him here."

He heard Lucy turn. "You lie."

"No, I don't. He'll come if he thinks there's a chance to save his mother. He doesn't know your true intentions."

"What do you think?" Lucy asked Mrs. Windsor.

"He's probably right. Once he sees all that you've done, he'll understand."

Luke knew Mrs. Windsor trusted him to speak to Christian and have the cavalry come riding in. *Not exactly, my dear.*

"They'll trace the call," Lucy said.

"Not if you use my phone. My personal one is encrypted."

Lucy's face was contorted in thought, deciding whether to trust him.

"If y-y-you're luh-lying, I'll cuh-cut your tongue out."

"Did you grab my phone when you kidnapped me?"

"It's in the cuh-cuh-car," Lucy said.

"Bring it here."

She stood slowly and walked to him. She looked at him for a few seconds, casting her final judgment on his suggestion. Finally, she turned and lifted the door, before slipping under it.

"He'll save us, won't he?" Mrs. Windsor whispered.

"Quiet now."

It only took the Priestess a minute or so to grab the phone and come back in, closing the door behind her. She walked to Luke and put the phone to his face. "H-he's under Cuh-cuh-Christian?"

"Yes." The phone was already ringing.

"Luke?"

"It's me, Christian."

"Where are you?" Windsor's voice was low, as if he was in a movie theater. Luke heard no emotion.

"I'm with her."

Lucy pulled the phone away from his face, looked at it for a second, and then clicked the speakerphone on.

"She can hear you now," Luke said.

"Is my mother there? Veronica?"

"We're all here," Luke said.

"Let me hear their voices."

"I'm here, Christian," his mother said.

"Veronica is unconscious," Luke said.

Christian was quiet for a few seconds. "What's your name?" he said to the Priestess.

Her eyes widened and her face froze completely still with the shock that her savior was speaking to her taking over.

"Her name is Lucy, Christian. She wants you to come here to us. She wants to show you what she's been planning for you."

"Tell me where you are, Lucy," Christian said in that same low voice. Luke liked the sound of it. Perhaps he wasn't emotionless. Maybe rage rested beneath, unlike the fear he normally carried around.

"N-n-no."

"Then how can I come to you?"

"I-I-I'll come to yuh-yuh-you," she said.

"When?"

Luke looked at Lucy and saw she was considering how this would work. She wasn't good at thinking on her feet. She needed time to process—or talk to God, whichever she preferred to call it. Right now, there wasn't time to ask God what to do.

"Soon," she said and hung up the phone. She put it in her pocket and then looked at Luke. "You're luh-luh-lying. If I tell him, cops will come. A l-l-l-lot of them. But Muh-muh-Mrs. Windsor is right. I need to buh-buh-bring him here."

"You'll need me, if you want to get him without being caught," Luke said. "You'll need to grab him at the office when it's late and no one's working. He's being watched now, because of how you grabbed Veronica. You won't be able to sneak into someone's house again."

Lucy looked down at her watch. Luke knew the time, though he hadn't seen a clock in days. It was nearing four in the morning.

"When?" she said.

"Tomorrow night. Around this time."

"Okay," she said.

Luke expected her to leave, to need time away from him so that she could pray—the psychopath's way of dealing with the world around her. Luke, for once, was wrong. She sat down in front of Christian's mother and began talking again.

Luke closed his eyes.

He needed to be near Christian. He needed a chance to talk with him. Christian's rebirth was near. The boy only needed a nudge in the right direction.

---

Tommy reached out to knock on Christian's door, but his partner opened it before his knuckles connected.

Christian's gun was holstered on his hip.

"Let's go," he said, passing by Tommy.

"Where to?"

"The office."

"Why didn't we just meet there, then?"

Christian reached Tommy's car and turned around. "Because we need to talk first. When we get there we need to work."

Tommy saw the intensity that had been missing in

Christian for months. The part that arrived when his brain moved at full speed, functioning like a supercomputer.

Tommy went to the car, unlocked the doors, and they both got in.

"I was right. The person doing this is a woman," Christian said.

"How do you know?"

"She called me from Luke's phone, or rather, she allowed Luke to call me—"

"When?"

"Just be quiet, Tommy. Let me talk."

Tommy looked over but Christian kept his gaze straight ahead. "Okay, go on."

"She's coming to get me. She wants me to witness what she's going to do to them. They're alive for now. We're going to let her come get me, and when she does, you'll let her take me. Then you follow, and once we arrive, you'll send in the tactical team."

"Then why are we going to the office? If she's coming, we can set this all up from your house."

"No," Christian said, shaking his head. "No one else is involved. You're the only one who's going to follow her."

"Why?"

"Because other people could fuck it up. You won't. I won't. *Our* friend is there. Other people don't have anyone they love involved. You follow and when you understand where we're going, then you call reinforcements."

Tommy drove down the road, not speaking for a second. "I still don't understand why we're going to the office."

"Luke is smart. He'll know to tell her to go there because we'll be working on catching her."

"Are we?"

"We don't have to. You stay alert. I have to go back to my mansion."

They finished the ride in silence, with Tommy contemplating all the rules they were breaking. When Waverly found out, they'd all lose their jobs. Hell, they'd probably lose them even if everyone survived.

None of that really mattered, though. Christian was right. They had to save those they loved. Tommy had to decide whether Christian's plan was the one with the greatest chance of success, or whether emotion was ruling his normally logical thought process.

Christian went to his office and turned on the computer. He sat down in front of the light, leaving the rest of the floor in darkness. Tommy found a corner and sat down in it, putting his ass on the floor. He wanted to stay out of the light in case she came tonight.

What if she didn't?

He stood and walked back across the floor.

"What if she doesn't show up?"

Christian opened his eyes. "Then we wait until she does."

Tommy nodded, supposing he could use the days to do actual investigative work. He turned and went back to his corner. Tommy watched Christian's eyes close again, and wondered if they were making a mistake.

He couldn't know what was going on inside Christian's head, but he knew the world. He knew the FBI. Could other agents fuck it up if they were involved? Sure. Could he and Christian handle all of this on their own?

He didn't know.

It was only one woman, but that single woman had disabled one of the most capable agents Tommy knew. She'd then killed two cops on her way to kidnapping her fifth person.

*Shit, this broad is crazy. She's like the fucking Terminator.* Tommy chuckled. He almost couldn't believe it was a woman. Not in a sexist way.

He stared at Christian until just before the sun rose, unable to make up his mind. When he heard the elevator open on the floor, he got to his feet. Just the first employee coming in, someone wanting to get a jump on the day.

Tommy walked to Christian's office. "Hey," he said, unsure how loud he should be.

Christian opened his eyes and a chill went through Tommy as he spoke. "I'm going to kill her."

---

Tommy had spent the small hours of the morning staring at Christian.

Christian had spent the same time staring at the girl who considered him next to God. That, and listening to the voice inside his head. The one that said it was *him*, or what he would become. Perhaps it told the truth. Christian wasn't sure any longer. He only knew he had to get his mother back. Veronica and Luke, too.

Two years ago, when he'd watched Bradley Brown's life play out in his head, he'd felt pity for the man. Not empathy, exactly, but perhaps sympathy for what he'd gone through. That sympathy was what created the few moments of space for Luke to step in and kill Brown.

Now, as he watched this girl, not a single thought of sorrow moved through him. His mind had turned cold against her, becoming a calculating thing with very little difference from a machine.

He'd watched the girl learn how to strangle herself in order to induce hallucinations.

*If you won't allow her to serve you, you're going to have to kill her. You know that right?* the Other, as Christian was coming to think of the voice, had said.

He'd watched the girl whip her back with a large leather strap, repenting for perceived transgressions.

*You want to kill her, Christian. If you're being honest with yourself,* the Other had said.

He'd listened to the girl's father preach about the Lord and how he would send a message dictating who their savior would be.

*She's going to kill everyone you love if you let her,* the Other had said.

Christian hadn't responded, but it seemed to speak a truth that he'd been ignoring. No, *refusing* to hear because of its ruthlessness.

In the end, as his mind's video showed the girl writhing in pain from another parental "lesson," the Other was all he heard, whispering sweet nothings of revenge.

"Hey," Agent Bench said at the entrance to Christian's office.

Christian's chair was turned around and he was looking out his office window. He'd been out of his mansion for some time, but there was no need to do any actual work. Everything would be finished soon.

Christian swung his chair and faced Bench.

"Hey, what's up?"

"Got a second?"

"Sure," Christian said.

Bench approached his desk but didn't sit down. He handed him a piece of paper that showed a license plate, a name, and a car model.

"A local cop found this car late last night in a ditch. It wasn't far from Luke's house, and it's been impounded. I'm swamped dealing with these search warrants, would you or Tommy mind looking at it?"

Christian viewed the picture of the early model car. It was from the nineties, and the owner's name said it belonged to a Wesley Speckle. It made sense. The Priestess showed up in her car, but why not take Luke's instead?

"Yeah, I'll take care of it."

"Thanks a lot. These judges are a beast with the warrants."

"No problem," Christian said.

"All right, I'll stop by later." Bench turned and walked out of the room, leaving Christian with the paper that would lead him to the Priestess. He looked at it for a few seconds, then folded it up and stuck it in his desk drawer.

There was no need for it.

The Priestess would come for him, and then, he'd end all of this. No reason to get anyone else involved.

Christian sat back down in his chair and continued staring out of his office window.

———

Tommy was getting tired, yet he knew sleep was a luxury he wouldn't see for a long time.

He had tried checking in on Christian throughout the day, but the kid wanted nothing to do with Tommy—or anyone, apparently. He stared at his computer screen, rapidly typing on the keyboard.

"What are you doing?" Tommy asked.

"Working."

"Want to let me in on the kind of work you're doing?"

"No," Christian said.

Tommy didn't like the look on his face and as the day wore on, he began rethinking their decision to do this alone. Another twelve hours had passed, and they knew nothing more about Luke's, or anyone else's, condition.

Bench came by Tommy's office, and despite Tommy's penchant for long hours and hard work, he was staring blankly at an empty web browser.

"Hey," Bench said from the door.

Tommy looked up and blinked. "Hey."

"You sleep at all last night?"

"Not much," Tommy said.

"I gave Windsor something to work on a little while ago, might not be anything important. He seemed kind of out of it, so I didn't stay long. Either of you heard anything?"

This was his chance to let the world in on Christian's plan. All he needed to say was, "Yeah, she's coming for Christian next," and yet Tommy couldn't bring himself to say the words.

Instead, he shook his head.

"All right. I'm going to start making calls. We're speaking with Waverly at noon. He wants an update on the warrants."

Tommy nodded, and as Bench left, he went back to his computer screen. He had put all this in Christian's hands. A twenty-five-year-old kid who'd never used his weapon in the line of duty.

For the second time, he walked down to Christian's office. He went straight to his desk without knocking. He touched the screen's button, turning it black.

Christian looked at him with a cool, even stare, as if the human behind them had been replaced with a machine running infinite calculations.

"If she doesn't come tonight," Tommy said, ignoring the frightening thoughts Christian's face brought to mind, "we're telling Bench and Waverly. I'll give this one more night, but what we're doing is colossally idiotic."

Christian nodded. "She'll come tonight."

# CHAPTER TWENTY-TWO

Luke had to adjust the car seat, and it annoyed him to no end that this *Priestess* had rearranged it in the first place. He said nothing, though, as Lucy pointed a gun at him from the passenger seat.

It was one in the morning and the two of them were heading to the Atlanta FBI office. Lucy was extremely careful, which fit someone with her deficiencies. If your face jumped around like a cricket on a hot stove, you couldn't afford a bunch of other mess-ups in life. You needed to be able to look at the world around you and see danger before it arrived.

She was doing that well. Mrs. Windsor might not understand Luke's nature, nor Veronica's, but Lucy had no problem with it. Delusional about Christian, she might be, but not about Luke.

"If you do anything I don't like, I'll shoot you through the ribs," she said as the car started.

"We'll both die, then, as it will be pretty hard to control the vehicle with a bullet lodged in my lungs."

"God's on my side. You're the only one who'll die."

"Fair enough," Luke said and pulled the car from the parking lot. He looked around him, amazed at how little the world paid attention. They weren't in as populated an area as downtown Atlanta, but this storage unit wasn't in the middle of nowhere either. Sure, they were in the back of a five hundred unit place that appeared to be spread out over quite a number of acres, but there was a gas station a mile down the road.

Lucy, and Luke to a lesser extent, were allowed to exist because of humanity's refusal to glance up from their phones. To look around the world and *notice* what was right in front of them. Like someone about to be crucified upside down.

"What do you think God will do with Christian?" Luke asked as the car entered the highway.

"It's nuh-none of your concern."

"I disagree. If I am what you say I am, I think I have a great deal of concern here."

He glanced over at her. Her upper lip was twitching. She never noticed any of it, not any more than someone noticed breathing. It was simply a part of her.

"Christian is going to wipe all evil from the Earth."

"Is he the Second Coming?"

"You're a heathen."

"Your stutter disappears when you're focused, Lucy," Luke said.

The girl turned her head slightly and looked out the front window. Her body and the weapon remained pointed at Luke.

"Nuh-no. He's not the second coming. He is the person

that will pave the way for Jesus's return. The Lord won't return if there is evil here. It's an affront to Him."

"Do you think Christian will take part in my crucifixion?"

"If he realizes what he is in time. If not, that's o-okay. Now stuh-stop talking."

Luke did as he was told for twenty minutes or so, the sound of the wheels rolling over the pavement filling the car.

"What if Christian decides you're evil, Lucy? What if it's you he wipes off the Earth?"

"He won't. God won't let him."

Luke watched her gnaw on her lower lip as the thought he introduced wormed its way into her mind. The inherent evil her father hoisted on her as a child rearing its head, telling her she wasn't worthy of God or the sword he'd made in Christian.

"That's good. Because if he were to turn his righteous anger on you, there wouldn't be much you could do, right?"

"Stuh-stuh-stop talking," the Priestess said.

Luke drove the rest of the way in silence, having done what he needed. The highway street lights moved over-head, briefly illuminating the dark car as it passed beneath them. Luke's brown eyes never moved from the road.

Thirty minutes later, they arrived at their destination. Luke pulled the car into the parking deck, flashing his credentials at the card reader. Tomorrow, if anyone cared to look, they'd see that Luke Titan had arrived at 2:01 in the morning. Luke wondered briefly what they would think.

It didn't matter. He would define the story.

He surveyed the surroundings but saw nothing alarming. Christian was playing his role in this, the one that Luke had begun creating years ago. He wanted to be found now, just as Luke had a few days ago. Tommy was here, too. Unfortunate for him.

"How do we get in?" Lucy said.

"Take the elevator down then cross the street. We have to go in through the main entrance."

"I'll kill you before I let you do something that could get me arrested."

"I know, Lucy. That's not what I want, for either of us. I think that what you're doing is going to turn into something very beautiful. I want to see it." Luke didn't face her as he spoke.

He looked through the parking deck to the FBI building. He could see inside Christian's office. A light was on, and Christian was sitting with his eyes closed in front of his computer.

Luke's vision was closer to that of an eagle's than a human's.

*What's talking to you right now, Christian?* he wondered.

"Move," the Priestess said.

Luke took her down the stairs and across the street. She walked close enough to him to hide the weapon. Luke felt it digging into his side. He stopped on the sidewalk, just before the stairs that led to the entrance.

"No one is in the lobby, but there are cameras throughout the building. There is a single private security guard monitoring them, but most nights he dozes."

"How do you know?"

"I've watched him," Luke said. He had, sometimes for

hours, just standing behind the twenty-something-year-old security guard while he slept with his head on the desk. "Even so, the lights are on in the lobby and you'll want to hide the weapon until we're past them. The floor we're going to will have its lights off, and the cameras won't pick anything up. You can point it back at me, then."

He still didn't look at her, but he felt the gun disappear from his ribcage.

Luke used his ID card to enter the lobby.

The two moved through the lobby quickly and stepped into the elevator.

He felt the gun press against his body again.

"What's your plan, Lucy? Are you going to use me as leverage against him, to ensure he comes with you?"

She looked forward.

"What if he's got surveillance here, Lucy? What if he's being watched?"

Luke waited until he saw her start chewing her lip. The girl was very quick, but Luke moved like a viper. His elbow connected with her temple, her body and the gun falling simultaneously, hitting the floor at roughly the same time.

Luke hit the button for three floors below Christian's.

---

Tommy's eyes were closing on him. He sat in the same corner as he had the previous night, but now his head kept threatening to fall against his chest, letting sleep storm the beach of his mind.

Tommy stood up and slapped himself across the face. He looked at his watch for what felt like the millionth time.

Only five minutes had passed. The night was stretching on forever as if the Earth had stopped revolving.

He looked into Christian's office from where he stood. Tommy had suggested leaving the light on inside, so that if anyone did come, their eyes would naturally be drawn there, making it easier for Tommy to hide.

Tommy didn't so much see the shadow, as feel it. He moved fast, his right arm striking out, palm open, trying to slam into the nose of whoever stood next to him.

His eyes were somewhat blind, his pupils too dilated from staring at Christian's bright office.

Someone grabbed his hand, the grip feeling like steel clamping on his bones. Tommy's left hand shot up in a fist, but his right arm was already twisting, turning painfully and forcing the rest of Tommy's body to turn as well.

His left fist swung hopelessly in the wrong direction. Tommy kicked behind him, even as his wrist was pinned against his back.

"*Christian!*" he shouted just before he felt an infinitely strong arm wrap around his neck. He tried to pull at it with his left hand, but the attacker didn't budge. The muscles across the bicep and forearm were brutally strong.

Finally, Tommy lost consciousness and sagged toward the ground, his assailant the only thing holding him up.

---

Christian opened his eyes, the scream penetrating his mansion and breaking through the movies playing there.

He looked out of his office but saw nothing. The lights from above blinded him to whatever waited outside.

"Tommy?" he called, his voice carrying through the empty floor.

No answer returned.

*She's here.*

But how did she overpower Tommy? How did she even know where he was?

It didn't matter. Tommy wasn't answering, so she must have found and disabled him.

"Come on then," Christian said quietly.

He waited but nothing moved outside. If he wanted to turn the lights on, he would have to cross the floor, as they all sat on the other side. Which meant he had to go practically blind into the darkness.

*What are you waiting for?*

It wasn't his mother who spoke. Or his shrink. It was the Other.

*You've wanted her to come. She's here. Go to her.*

Christian turned halfway around and saw himself standing there. The other version's hands were at his sides, covered in blood that dripped to the floor, landing quietly on the carpet.

*Go on,* the Other said, a smile on his face.

Christian turned back around and walked out of the room. He turned the lights off as he moved through the doorway, pitching the whole place in blackness. He stopped walking at the first cubicle, letting his eyes adjust. He pulled his weapon from the holster. He would kill her now if he got the chance, anything to keep her away from his mother.

"I'm here. Let's get this over with."

"Christian, it's me." Luke's voice came from the other

end of the floor, and though Christian turned his head in that direction, he couldn't pinpoint it. "She says to put the gun down. She has one pointed at me."

Christian squinted, hoping to see *something*, but even though he could make out the cubicle shapes easily, he saw nothing resembling another person.

He set the gun down next to him, knowing that he was breaking protocol by doing so. What did that matter though, when this whole enterprise was a break in protocol?

"What do I do, Luke?"

"Don't struggle."

Christian couldn't tell if it was Luke talking or the voice from inside his head, the whisper in his ear so close and hot, with no warning. He felt the same strong arm that Tommy had, it wrapping around his throat like a boa constrictor.

And then, he found himself in sweet darkness, just as Tommy had.

For the second time since they met, Luke stood above Christian's limp body.

The world would say it wasn't fair, the gifts bestowed upon Luke while so many others struggled simply to get along. Of course, they didn't understand the responsibilities that came with such talent. No one did, except for Luke. And now he had to fulfill a part of said responsibility.

He reached down and grabbed Christian's legs, then

pulled him across the floor to the other two bodies he'd collected.

Jesus was a fisher of men. Luke was a collector of bodies. Was there any difference? Doesn't a fisher use a hook and lure to capture his prey, and doesn't he consume them once they're dead? Luke would consume these people, too, though not their flesh.

"All right," he said. "Who's first?"

# CHAPTER TWENTY-THREE

Christian found himself on a green pasture.

A song was playing, though he saw no speakers. The song was *Strange Fruit*, an old one by Billie Holiday. It echoed out across the land as if a chorus of croaky angels sang from on high.

Christian looked up to see if there were any mythical creatures flying above but he saw none.

Still, the song continued.

Christian turned around. He saw Tommy on one side of the field and Luke on the other. He wanted to yell to them, but couldn't. His mouth wouldn't move, and it was then he realized he was dreaming.

He looked down at his feet and saw they were bare, and that there was blood on them. The blood was rubbing off on the blades of grass he stood on. When he looked back up, he saw his mother standing in front of him. Veronica was to her left, and behind both of them was the woman. He saw her face now, for the first time. Her hair was long and thin, parts of it messy and sticking out from the rest.

Her eyebrows and lips twitched as if an electrical current ran through her skin.

"You see her because, now, you know her," the voice said from behind Christian. He didn't need to turn around to know who it was. Himself. Or the version living inside his head.

The Other was right, though. He did know the woman, fully. He had learned her life the past evening, and now…

"Now it's time to play God, isn't it? Because God giveth and he taketh away. You've given her hope in life, and now it's time to take that life."

Christian looked to his right and saw Tommy, then to his left where Luke was standing. He didn't understand why Luke wasn't here with these three, another victim of this girl. He also didn't understand why his partners were so far away from each other.

Christian turned around and looked at the Other. Blood dripped from the corners of his mouth and when the Other started laughing, Christian saw that his mouth was full of blood. It fell down his chin, splattering on his t-shirt.

The Other kept laughing as if the blood pouring from his mouth was the funniest thing he'd ever seen.

---

Christian awoke, his body attempting to jerk free but the binds on his legs and arms kept him from moving.

"Calm down."

Christian didn't move. His mind immediately began

categorizing the entire scene before him. Closed space. Dark. At least one person was next to him. Luke's voice.

"Where is she?" Christian asked.

"I don't know."

"Where are we?"

"In my trunk," Luke said.

"Tommy?"

"No idea. I woke up here a little bit ago. I tried waking you, but you were out."

Christian swallowed and his throat lit up with fire as he did. He let out a groan, but that only stoked the flames.

"She choked you?"

Christian just nodded, hoping that Luke would feel the motion. He didn't want to speak again.

"Me too," Luke said.

A minute passed in silence and then Christian managed, "We're not moving."

"No, we've been stopped since I woke."

"My mother?"

"She's fine."

"Veronica?" Christian asked.

"She was unconscious but breathing. I think she took a pretty hard beating."

Christian's teeth gritted together. "What is *she* planning?"

"She'll crucify me upside down and make you watch. I'm sure you've figured out she thinks you're basically Jesus Christ. Or, if not him, then his harbinger."

"Yes."

"How did she do this?" Christian said. "Five of us. She took five of us, plus killed another two cops."

Luke chuckled. "Maybe God is on her side. Or something close to his stature. What was your plan? You and Tommy were just going to wait for her to show up and then stop her?"

"She was supposed to take me, and Tommy was going to follow. We didn't think she'd get the jump on both of us. Sexism, I suppose."

Luke laughed again. "It gets the best of us all from time to time."

Christian rolled over on his side, his body nearly in a ball. He couldn't see anything. Only darkness resided in this trunk. "We've got to figure out how to kill her."

"Is that what you want to do?"

"Yes. We have to," Christian said.

"Why?"

"What the hell are you talking about? We're lying in the back of your trunk and she kidnapped my mother. Not to mention you and your patient. Now she's got Tommy, too." Christian's voice grew louder as he spoke, the rage inside threatening to spill out before it could be put to good use.

"We could capture her, Christian. She doesn't have to die."

Christian shook his head, not understanding what the fuck Luke was thinking. "She dies."

"Okay."

They lay in silence so pervasive that Christian thought he heard Luke's lips sliding over his teeth. "Are you smiling?"

"Shh," he said. "Here she comes."

The trunk opened and light poured in. A woman stood

above, looking like a thin ghost. One with a large bruise on the side of her head.

She held a crowbar in her right hand. She looked at Christian for a moment then brought the crowbar up with both hands. She slammed it on top of Luke's head. The crack echoed in the close quarters.

"Thuh-thuh-thuh-there," she said, then looked at Christian with the biggest smile he'd ever seen.

———

Veronica looked at Tommy Phillips. His mouth was taped shut just like hers. The only person in this place allowed to speak, apparently, was Christian's mother, who sat on the opposite side of Veronica.

She was tied in the same manner as Veronica, with her arms bound in front.

Tommy was tied differently than both of them, his arms around his back like Veronica, but attached to his bound feet as well, twisting him in a way that looked awfully painful. He wasn't conscious yet.

Veronica had watched the woman drag him in, surprised at how easily she'd moved him. What the hell was she doing? Collecting everyone Christian knew?

She almost couldn't believe she'd found herself in a spot like this again. She supposed this was her own fault, in a very humorous and fucked up way. She kept hanging out with people who dealt with psychopaths for a living.

"I wonder what she's doing," Christian's mother said.

Veronica turned to look at her but could only shake her

head. This all seemed too surreal to be true. It couldn't *possibly* be happening again.

"That Luke fellow. She's going to crucify him upside down, I think," Mrs. Windsor said. "She doesn't like you too much, either. I think I'm going to make it out of this, though. She seems to be a fan of mine." The older woman smiled, and Veronica realized she was only half joking. "She thinks I'm basically Mother Mary, a Saint in her eyes. Are you Christian's girlfriend?"

Despite her fear, Veronica would have smiled if there wasn't tape across her face. She nodded.

"I know this doesn't bode well for your relationship, but if you make it out of this, try not to think too harshly about him. He doesn't have any other ex-girlfriends like this, I promise."

Veronica laughed into the tape and tears came to her eyes. She saw they were in the older woman's as well, and they started crying and laughing together.

Both stopped seconds later when the padlock moved outside the closed door.

The woman opened it all the way for the first time. She tossed Luke in. Blood was leaking from the top of his head, over his ear, and onto his chin. *A lot* of blood. A horrible bruise combined with a swelling knot had risen on his skull, right where the blood stemmed from.

His body bounced slightly as he hit the floor and then remained still. Veronica could see him still breathing, but that was the only sign of life Luke gave.

Next, the woman walked Christian in. She moved him slowly, almost gingerly, since Christian had to hop with the way his legs were tied. He squinted to block out the overhead light. He didn't appear hurt, although his legs and arms were bound the same way as Luke's, which were the same as Veronica's, but different than Tommy's.

The three of them all had their arms in front of them. Only Tommy was tied in that acrobatic state.

Veronica's eyes found the woman, and she was smiling as she guided her savior.

"You're going to luh-love this, Christian. I just know it."

# THE BOOK OF TITAN

# CHAPTER TWENTY-FOUR

Luke's mind went black for a period of time, though he didn't know how long. It slowly woke, even if he remained unconscious. While the human brain doesn't operate like a computer, the best way to understand Luke's is through that comparison.

His mind began a system check first, trying to understand what was wrong with the body it controlled. Though conscious thought would later label the injury to his skull as a fracture, his mind immediately recognized the damage. The fact that it could perform the system check revealed that there wasn't any swelling of the brain, which was the most dangerous threat for someone like Luke Titan.

His mind did finally wake him, and as consciousness took hold, he didn't open his eyes. He didn't move at all or make a single sound. He remained motionless in the same way he'd been while unconscious.

Someone was dragging him across the floor, and from the feel of the hand, he knew it to be Lucy. The Priestess.

She clearly wasn't happy with what he'd done to her earlier.

She should be thankful. He'd wrapped everything up in a bow, just as he had with Bradley Brown.

After subduing Christian, Luke had tied him up, then Tommy. He'd killed the security guard, then carefully erased all data from the security systems before shutting them down. Next, he'd carried Tommy over one shoulder and Christian over the other, and placed Tommy in the back seat. Luke's strength was most comparable to that of an ant, although he wasn't capable of lifting something ten times his body weight. The limitations weren't with his muscles, but his skeletal structure. His bones would break under the pressure.

Tommy was bound well enough that he wouldn't be able to attack Lucy on the way to the storage unit. Luke had dropped Christian in the trunk and then went to Lucy. He wrote a brief note and pinned it to her.

*Go to the car. Everything is ready.*

*- The Demon*

He had returned to the car and bound his legs, and then his arms. Then he'd hopped into the trunk next to Christian before closing it behind himself.

As he awoke, his talk in the trunk with Christian came back to him.

It had been productive. It had shown Luke the boy was where he wanted him mentally.

Luke had predicted his own current state, although perhaps not the brutality of Lucy's attack. She certainly wanted to make sure Luke had no more chances to disable her.

He felt his arm being tied down to a piece of wood. The woman pulled tight on the metal wire and his bones creaked under its pressure. His other arm was next to be strapped to the cross that the woman had built. Luke's head slumped to the side, as though he were still unconscious.

He listened for more movement but heard none. Christian and the rest were still. No one was speaking.

It was time.

Luke opened his eyes and let out a slight groan. The pain in his head was extravagant, or it should have been. Luke's control over his own mind was such that while he felt the pain, his body followed his refusal to allow it to affect him. The groan was little more than acting.

He blinked a few times, seeing everything he needed immediately, but keeping up the charade.

He lay horizontal on the large cross. The bucket of dried cement was about a foot from his head, lying on its side with the cross stuck inside it. Lucy had been a busy beaver.

"Christian," the Priestess said. "I know you don't understand yet, but this is all for you. I think you will gih-gih-get it after I'm finished. Your muh-mother already does."

Luke looked at Christian sitting against the wall in between his mother and girlfriend. His mouth wasn't taped shut like Veronica's and Tommy's. He didn't say anything, but his eyes found Luke. No recognition of what had happened rested in them, so it seemed Lucy hadn't spoken about the FBI office.

Perhaps she didn't want her savior to know how badly she had messed up.

Christian's face was stone, and Luke appreciated that. For the first time in the boy's life, he was seeing horrible things and not showing emotion. Luke knew he *felt* emotions right now. The primary one being rage.

"Hi, again, Lucy," Luke croaked. "How are you?"

"Buh-buh-better than you," she stuttered.

Luke chuckled.

The woman moved to the cross and with both hands, pushed up the two hundred plus pounds. Luke hung upside down, his body immediately sagging toward the floor, the pull on his shoulder joints beginning at once.

"How are you, Veronica?" Luke said, forcing a smile onto his face as blood rushed to his fractured head.

She began crying.

"It's okay. I promise. It'll all be okay. Isn't that right, Lucy?"

"Not for either of you." The Priestess turned around and looked at Veronica. "I haven't decided what to do with her yet."

"I'm sure you'll work it out," Christian said.

Lucy took a step back.

"This is what you think I want?" Christian continued. "My friends and loved ones tied up and ready to die?"

It didn't take a genius to understand the route that Christian would take. It was also the one Luke planned on.

"It's fuh-for y-y-you," Lucy said, her voice cracking.

"Did you even ask me what I wanted?"

Lucy's head shook back and forth in tiny movements. She wasn't saying no, but couldn't understand what was happening and that was simply her body's reaction.

"No, you didn't, Lucy. You never even thought to ask.

Do you think you know better than I do, as to what should happen?"

"Wuh-wuh-what are you talking about?"

"*Quit stuttering!*" Christian's voice erupted through the enclosed space, his rage spilling out into the world like black, flaming oil.

Lucy whimpered and took another step back.

Christian pushed himself against the wall, then pushed himself up so that he stood. His legs were bound far too tightly for him to walk, but he leaned against it with his hands in front of him.

"Untie me."

Lucy shook her head.

"*Untie me!*"

"I cuh-cuh-can't. Not until I'm finished with him. You have to see it fuh-fuh-first."

Christian looked down at the floor, and when he spoke, his voice was death personified. "If you don't untie me now, when you're finished, I will kill you in the most horrific possible fashion."

Lucy tried to interrupt, but Christian kept going without looking up. "No. Let me tell you what I'll do. I will slice your tongue in two so that you can still try and speak, but your language will make your stutter appear like a gift. I'll take your skin off slowly, over the course of days, and staple your eyelids to your skull so that you have to watch. You'll finally die as another disciple did. I'll boil you in a vat of oil. Either free me, or your fate will be worse than the man you're crucifying."

Lucy's head shook so fast it was almost vibrating.

Luke watched it all, highly interested, but still dispassionate. This was only the beginning.

Lucy bolted toward the open door. Once outside, she pulled it down, and Luke heard the padlock slam into place.

Luke closed his eyes and let out another groan.

---

Christian watched the door slide down and listened as the woman locked them all inside. He turned to Luke.

"Hold on." He hopped carefully over to the cement bucket that held Luke suspended in the air. "This is going to hurt."

"It's been a day of hurt," Luke said.

Christian lowered his shoulder at the wooden cross and shoved hard. The bucket started to tip, but it remained upright. Christian leaned on the cross and fell with it.

The sound of the wood hitting the concrete echoed off the surrounding metal walls. Christian rolled off Luke's arm and stared up at the ceiling.

"Mom, are you okay?"

"I'm okay, honey. Dr. Titan is the one hurting, I think."

"Veronica?" Christian said. "How about you?"

He looked at her and saw her nod.

"Tommy is still out?" Christian couldn't see him from where he lay.

"It appears so, honey," his mother said.

Christian let out a sigh. "That didn't go like I wanted."

"It went better than the alternative," Luke said. "At least I'm not hanging upside down anymore."

"What do you think she's doing?" Mrs. Windsor asked.

Christian didn't know, hadn't even given himself time to consider it. He had lost himself for a moment while screaming at the woman, threatening her. It had been...

*Exhilarating.*

Christian saw the Other standing next to him. His eyes were black, and he still smiled as if someone had hooked the corners of his lips to his ears, stretching them much wider than could possibly be sustained. Blood pattered around Christian's head and landed on the floor.

Some of it splattered against his face. Christian didn't care.

"What are you looking at?" Luke said.

"Nothing."

"Are you sure?"

Christian turned his head to the side and found Luke staring at him.

*Does he know?*

Luke knew something. His face said as much.

Tommy groaned, and Christian rolled on his side, kicking his legs so that he could see his other partner.

"Tommy? You awake?"

Tommy let out another groan, and Christian saw him try to speak. The tape across his mouth kept him from doing so. They all sat in silence as he slowly worked it off, scraping his face against the ground until the tape peeled away. Road rash set across his cheeks, but he gave no sign of the pain.

"What the fuck happened?" Tommy slurred.

"She's got us."

Tommy looked around the room, seeing the other people here with him. "Luke, you okay?"

"I've had better days."

Tommy groaned again. He couldn't sit up with the way his arms were tied to his legs, couldn't move much at all. "Where is she?"

"She just left," Christian said. His face was pressed against the ground and he realized that he'd rolled into a puddle of blood. Not Luke's or his own, but the dripping apparition's.

*She'll be back*, the Other said. *She's probably praying to God, and when she's done, she'll kill everyone you love.*

Christian tried not to look up. He didn't want Luke seeing it, or anyone else for that matter. This apparition was no different from the times his mother or shrink showed up to offer advice. He had to ignore it.

"Do we have a plan?" Tommy said.

"No," Christian answered.

*Yes, you do*, the Other said. *You know what you need to do. You've got to kill her, just like you've planned. Only, you might not be able to do it with* your *hands.*

The lights above went out for the first time, casting everyone into darkness.

# CHAPTER TWENTY-FIVE

Lucy didn't understand what was happening. A whirlwind of terror had erupted inside the storage unit with Christian's mouth as its source.

She knew God was pain. Daddy had taught her that, but was His sword also pain? Was *this* supposed to be happening?

Lucy had cut the lights off inside the storage unit, wanting them unable to see a thing. She knew it was dangerous leaving them *all* in there alone, but she didn't have any choice. She had to think, had to talk to God.

When Lucy started renting the unit, she had found the metal cord connecting the power source on the side of the building. She had left a pair of hedge cutters next to it some time ago, wanting to be prepared.

She snipped the cord, knowing it meant she wouldn't be able to turn the lights back on. That was fine. Their blindness was more important than her sight.

Lucy had heard the bucket topple over and knew that the demon was no longer facing his fate.

*Fate. Christian told you your fate would be worse than his, yet you didn't listen to him.*

Lucy stared at Titan's car, the moon above casting its glow off the smooth metal. She needed to get away from here, to find a place to pray. She would come back tomorrow night. *If* God spoke to her. If He did not, she would wait. Christian could bake in the heat just like the rest of them, and if they all died, then Lucy had been mistaken. If the cops showed up, then Lucy had been mistaken.

This was in God's hands until He gave her direction.

*Stop stuttering!*

Tears came to Lucy's eyes as she remembered Christian's harsh words. His *angry* words. Her father had said the same words to her so many times, and she had never been able to listen. She had never been able to stop.

Christian shouldn't talk like that. Maybe to others, he *was* the sword after all, but not to her. It made no sense.

Lucy got into the car and drove off. On her way home the sun rose, and she took some happiness in knowing that the temperature inside the storage unit would grow hotter. Perhaps they'd die and God would show her a different path. Perhaps Christian would melt in there.

*Don't think like that!*

She parked the car a mile from her apartment, not wanting anyone to see her driving something so expensive. She wanted no interruptions for what came next.

She walked to her apartment, the sun fully up now. She wanted to sleep but knew she couldn't. She first needed to seek God. Lucy wasn't going to work today and knew that meant she'd lose her job, but what did a job matter right now?

Lucy entered the apartment and went to the closet. She had bought the whip when she got the apartment but hadn't used it. How many years had it been since she and her father had taken something very similar across their backs? A decade, maybe?

Lucy undressed and folded her clothes before placing them on the bed. She knelt at the bed's foot, letting her bottom touch her heels. She brought the whip up in front of her and looked at it. It wasn't the cat-o-nine tails that she and her father had used, but Lucy knew that with her strength and enough focus, she could reach God.

She raised the whip in the air and slammed her arm across her chest, the leather strap slapping down on her back. Pain raged across her flesh, but she didn't slow down. She had to keep going.

Again the whip went up, and again it came down. Over and over, until she felt her back grow wet and her arm tired. Then, as Daddy had taught her, she switched arms and started again.

Finally, the pain grew too much, and her vision became hazy.

Lucy smiled as she fell to the side and blackness took over, allowing the God she believed in to enter her.

---

Hours passed in the darkness, but there was no doubt that the sun had risen outside. The heat crept up on Christian, and everyone else inside the small building, like a thief ready to steal the water from their bodies.

Christian hadn't moved at all but his shirt was soaked. Not only from the blood that still dripped from the Other's hands and mouth but because of his sweat, too.

Veronica had managed to scrape the tape from her mouth as Tommy had, using the concrete floor, but they all sat in silence. It was nearly too hot to talk.

"Christian," Luke said, his voice quiet but still able to be heard by all. "You awake?"

"Yes," he whispered.

"Tell me what you were looking at earlier."

Christian swallowed, his throat still hurting from the night before, but the pain had dulled some. "Nothing."

"You're lying. If it was nothing, you would have said you didn't know what I was talking about," Luke said.

No one else spoke.

"It's important, Christian. If you're hallucinating, it could mean severe dehydration."

"Honey, tell him," his mother said.

"I'm not hallucinating, Mom. Listen, Luke, ever since I was a boy, my mind has projected images of people when I'm feeling overwhelmed. You know what I'm talking about, Mom. That's all this is. Just an image."

Luke waited a few seconds and then said, "Of what?"

"It's not important."

"It is to me."

Christian gritted his teeth and felt the same rage he'd unleashed on Lucy trying to rise up. "I don't want to talk about it."

"Why?" Luke said.

"Because he doesn't, Luke. Let it drop," Tommy said from the other side of the room.

Christian didn't want anyone to know, because what he saw was insane. A bloodied, endlessly smiling version of himself who said sick things. Things he would never have considered before the goddamn voice showed up inside his head. To let someone know about it would let them see he was losing his mind.

*That's* why *you should tell someone,* Melissa said.

Christian couldn't see her in the darkness.

*No,* a deeper part of him said. *Don't say anything.*

A memory came back, of standing inside a former FBI agent's house and looking at Luke. The FBI agent was dead, as was his wife. The way Luke stared at the bodies had moved something inside Christian, leading him down a path to believing his partner was a murderer.

That same piece of Christian that warned him then was warning him now.

*Stop it,* he thought. *Just stop. You're dehydrated and kidnapped, so you're making up crazy fucking ideas that have no basis in reality.*

Perhaps that's what pushed him to speak. His will to trust Luke and ignore the only voice in the room that was truly his own.

Christian relaxed his jaw, realizing he was still grinding his teeth. He sighed. "It started six months ago. Around the time she got Goleen. Usually, when I see these things, it's either my mom or my therapist, and they try to steer me the right way. I know it's how my mind calms me down and gives me direction based on what it thinks they'd say, but it helps. Six months ago.

Jesus, this is a lot, Luke. Are you sure you want to hear it?"

"Yes."

"You know about the mansion in my head. I've told you about it. Well, six months ago a voice started talking to me inside it. I didn't know what it meant, only that it hadn't happened before. It shouldn't have been there. That mansion is mine, and for me. Not for anything else. But it wouldn't leave. I stopped going inside, and I think you and Tommy both know my work suffered. I was scared, but when she took you, I went back. I've been going back to keep learning about this fucking bitch, and the voice keeps talking. It's saying it's me."

He stopped, not wanting to go any further.

"Is it?" Luke asked.

"Who else could it be? It's in my head. Of course, it's me."

"Then what's the problem?" Veronica said.

Christian shook his head, although no one could see him. He didn't want her to hear this, perhaps more than anyone else in the room. His mother would love him no matter what, and his partners were his partners. Veronica could leave him at any moment. If any of them made it out of here alive.

*No, Christian. You shouldn't tell Luke.*

He threw the thought away.

"The problem is, the image my mind shows is *me*, but it's different. My hands are covered in blood. I'm smiling, and what I say, *that's* not me. It's not the things I think or believe."

"You know what I'm going to ask, don't you?" Luke

said.

"I don't want to talk about it anymore."

No one said anything for a moment, and then his mother spoke. "Honey, we don't have a lot going on in here, so maybe you could tell us just to keep our minds busy. Maybe Dr. Titan here can help you, or maybe your mind's trying to tell you what you should be doing."

Another push in the direction Christian didn't want to go. A push that he couldn't deny. His mother was his life.

"It's telling me to kill her. It's been telling me that she has to die for what she's done. She has to pay for this, for all of it. It's what I was talking about inside the trunk, Luke. That's what it's telling me."

"You don't think the voice is right?

"You asked me the same thing in the car, but you argued the other side."

"I wasn't tied to a cross at the time. It's changed my perspective some." Luke chuckled. "Why are you so against her death?"

"It's not that I'm against her dying. I'm against the *reason* I want her dead. It's vengeance. It's hate. That's not who I am."

"Sometimes situations dictate we change who we are, Christian. Do you remember what you did to Bradley Brown? You used his memories to change his actions, and it worked. It gave me time to get in there and stop him. Only, no one is coming this time. If you're going to save us, you might have to embrace those feelings. It might be the only way."

Tommy was silent in the dark room, listening to his two partners talk. Mrs. Windsor threw in a few cents every now and then, but he didn't pay much attention to her.

Luke's words were…different.

In fact, Luke was talking in a way that Tommy had never heard before. This might be the psychiatrist version of him that Tommy didn't know, but even so, it didn't feel right.

What he said made sense. If Christian could talk this psycho into freeing him, they'd have a chance at getting out of here. If Christian had to act a certain way for that to happen, then so be it, but Tommy didn't like it. He didn't like how Luke had driven the kid to talk when it was clear he didn't want to. During a time when they could have been planning an escape, and if not an escape, then something that might help when she returned, they were instead psychologically evaluating Christian.

But maybe that was what they needed to do, maybe that *was* the plan.

Tommy stopped thinking and spoke. "Look, we need to get an idea of what we're going to do when she returns. I've thought about chewing through the damn ropes, but it'll be impossible. They're too thick and our jaws would fail before we even got close."

The conversation between the two had ended a minute ago, and the room was silent again as everyone took in Tommy's words.

When Luke spoke, Tommy somehow felt that he'd been waiting a long time to say what he did.

"The only path out of this is if Christian embraces his mind. He's got to free us."

# CHAPTER TWENTY-SIX

Lucy woke up. Her head hurt, but not nearly as much as her back. She didn't move for quite some time, fearing the pain that would erupt when she did. She had felt this kind of pain before, but the fear of it was almost as bad as the actual hurt.

She looked out the window in her bedroom, a tiny thing, and saw that the sun was setting. She'd slept the entire day, but that was fine.

She'd seen Daddy in her dream, and she knew that the Lord had sent him to talk with her. Christian *was* the correct person, the sword that her tiny community had always believed in. He would bring destruction to the wicked.

Yet, he wasn't there *yet*, and that's what Daddy had shown her how to fix.

Momma hadn't been there yet. To be fair, she never made it, but Christian would. Lucy just had to teach him how to get there.

Lucy finally stood up and went to the mirror in her

bathroom. She turned around and looked over her shoulder to see the damage. It was bad. Blood caked her flesh. She needed bandages and antibacterial salve, but that would have to wait until tomorrow morning. Everything would be finished then. Lucy knew she only needed tonight.

Christian would learn the same way Lucy had, the same way her father had, and his before him. Through pain.

The Lord always taught His lessons through that medium.

---

Lucy arrived at the storage unit just after midnight. She hadn't wanted to show up any earlier since more of the town's people would be awake. Midnight, she figured, would see most of them at home in bed, giving her space and time to work.

She maneuvered the vehicle so that it faced the storage unit and kept its lights blaring. The unit wouldn't be *as* illuminated, but her solution should work.

Lucy brought the whip with her as she stepped from the car. She stood for just a second with the door open, deciding whether to bring the other thing. Even if she didn't use it, having it with her was better than not.

She reached back in and grabbed it from the passenger seat, then closed the door before walking to the unit. Using her key, she unlocked the padlock, took a step back, and pulled the pistol from her waistband.

She would need to do this quickly. If they had somehow managed to get loose, they'd be waiting to attack. The car lights would blind them, and her pistol would do the rest.

Lucy grabbed the door and flung it open with all her strength, her back crying out in angry protest. Ignoring it the best she could, Lucy jumped back and leveled the gun at the inside of the unit.

The car lights cast long shadows on the floor. A small sigh escaped her lips. Everyone was mostly in the same place she'd left them. The demon had fallen and was lying on the cross instead of hanging from it.

Lucy walked in and went to Christian. No one else mattered right now. Just him and his need to understand what he was supposed to be. She could deal with the rest later, once this matter was finished.

She knelt and set the gun behind her, making sure it was far enough away to avoid any possible tricks. She still held the whip.

"Cuh-Cuh-Cuh." Lucy paused, closed her eyes, and took a deep breath. When she opened them, she looked around the room again, seeing the other faces. Everyone was silent, all waiting on her to speak.

She brought her eyes back to Christian. "Hey." Another deep breath. "I know why you yuh-yelled at me earlier, and I'm not muh-mad about it."

Christian's eyes looked black in the gloomy lighting. He said nothing.

"I went and I prayed. God answers you when you honestly turn to Him. You just have to seek His will and not yuh-yuh-your own. Buh-before, I just wanted to see you anointed as His sword, but that isn't what God wants. Not at first. You must go through your trial by fire. You must be born again in the same way that I was, and Daddy, and everyone else. Then... Then, you'll see." Her eyes were wet. She hadn't spoken this much truth to anyone since Daddy died. "I know this is going to hurt. It's essential, though."

Lucy picked the whip up and wasted no time. She knew the order this would take.

She raised it high. Her back once again begged her to stop, but she paid it no mind. She slammed the whip down across Christian's chest.

He let out a loud scream, but Lucy barely heard it. The whip went up and then came down. Christian tried to move out of the way, squirming like a worm being toyed with by cruel children, but he couldn't escape. He couldn't resist God's holy trial.

Finally, he balled up and tried to block his face, but Lucy didn't care about that. His shoulders, his back, his chest, legs, or face. All of it was the same. All of it serving the Lord's greater purpose.

His screams didn't stop and neither did the ones coming from those around him. Everyone was begging her to stop, threatening to kill her, and on and on, like the heathens they were.

Christian didn't move at all. He lay there as the whip slapped against his wet shirt. In the poor lighting, Lucy couldn't tell if it was blood or sweat, but that was nonessential. Blood needed to be spilled. A lot of it.

"There," she said, losing her stutter totally in the moment. Christian was subdued and she needed him that way for what came next.

Lucy went to the back of the unit and grabbed the

metal wire she had used on Goleen and Titan. She walked it to the car and laid it next to the front wheel. When she returned to the unit, she paused and took in the mood. The screaming had stopped from the peanut gallery, and now she heard sobs.

They would cry harder before this ended.

She dragged Christian to the car and tossed him onto the hood. He landed hard, bending the metal beneath him. He lay still, his chest heaving.

Using the wire, she tied his hands to the side mirrors. Then, stretching the length of the wire, she bound his feet to the car's tires. He would be able to move some, but that was what the beating had been for. He wouldn't have enough energy to struggle.

She turned around and looked into the unit. One more thing.

Lucy walked to Titan and lifted his cross, so that he hung upside down, staring at Christian.

"Please," Mrs. Windsor said, her voice barely a whisper. "Please don't do this."

"When it's done, he'll be better for it, and so will you."

Lucy ignored the rest of the pleas and went to the car. She pulled the object from her pocket—a scalpel.

"You told me you would flay my skin, and when I prayed, God showed me how purposeful all your words are, Christian. You were showing me what I have to do to you, *to make you understand.*"

Christian felt as if his bones and muscle had turned to razor blades. He could barely move, and when he did, his body screamed with the fury of a thousand hurricanes.

He saw the Priestess standing above him, but barely heard anything she said. Her words were lost in the winds of pain soaring through his body.

Then she pulled something from her pocket.

Christian lifted his head slightly and saw the metal gleam beneath the moonlight. A scalpel. He dropped his head back, hitting the metal hard.

She walked toward him, her footsteps echoing in the silence. She lifted his shirt up. He didn't want to look down and see what she'd *already* done. The pain was enough.

Christian felt the first incision just above his right nipple. He let out a gasp, but he didn't scream.

*Well, what do you think? Are you going to let her skin you alive?*

Christian turned his head to the right and saw the other version of himself standing there. The blood that dripped from him was black in the moonlight. He had rolled his shirt sleeves up and Christian saw that the blood extended to his elbows, as if he had thrust both hands deep into a cow's exposed innards.

The scalpel cut across Christian's skin slowly, peeling back flesh with each millimeter Lucy moved it. Tears flooded Christian's eyes and he let out another gasp. Finally, the scalpel stopped moving and Christian forced himself to look.

The Priestess held a strip of his skin and blood flowed greedily across his torso, as if it wanted to cover every inch of him and wouldn't stop until it succeeded.

"I don't like doing this, but it's *essential*," the woman said. There was no emotion in her voice.

Christian's head fell against the car.

*You can make her kill herself right now, and you know it,* the Other said. *Just do it. Stop all of this.*

"Christian!"

He lifted his head again, hearing Luke's call. Luke's body sagged against the wires binding him.

"Listen to yourself," he said. "It's the only way."

"*Shut up, demon!*" Lucy screamed, whipping around to stare at Luke. He said nothing else and she turned back to Christian. "Are you beginning to see?"

Christian closed his eyes and made the decision.

"I see…a little girl…who can't stop stuttering," he whispered. "Do you see her?"

Lucy was standing over Christian again and had just slid the scalpel beneath his skin. She looked up but he didn't bother raising his head. His eyes remained closed as his mind fed him the necessary information.

"Tell me, Lucy, can you see her? Stuttering all the time. What did the kids in school do to you for it? Those were rough times weren't they?"

"Stop, Cuh-cuh-Christian. Stop. That's not fuh-fuh-funny."

"No, nothing was funny with those kids. Remember when your momma bought you that new dress, the first one your family had been able to afford all year, and they ripped it from your neck to your ass the first day you wore it to school? You were so proud of that dress, and they just reminded you that nothing you did would ever make you one of them."

He took a breath and felt the scalpel dig deeper, going past the upper layer of his skin.

"*Ssssstop!*"

Christian shook his head. "It was all because of your daddy. Him and his weird religion that only about five people in the whole fucking town believed in. All of them waiting on a sword to wipe out everyone else. A goddamn cult is what you were, and you knew it. Your mother knew it, too, but she was too goddamn weak to do anything. What about you, Lucy? You were the weakest. At some point, you started believing, didn't you?"

"*S-s-shut up!*"

The blade dug deeper, faster, and Christian groaned as he felt it touch his chest plate.

He didn't stop talking.

"You believed, and you've been waiting for that sword your whole life. Except no one else believed because no one else in the whole fucking…" He paused to catch his breath. "In the whole fucking country believed in that crazy shit. Now look at you, Lucy. Cutting me up for some God that doesn't fucking exist."

He raised his head and saw tears flowing down the woman's face. Rage built inside Christian as he spoke, replacing the fear and even some of the pain. As he watched her crying, he felt joy. Because *fuck her.*

*Fuck her,* the Other said next to him.

Or maybe the Other didn't say it at all. Maybe Christian spoke the words. He didn't know any longer.

"Your father never loved you. You were simply a tool to keep his crazy delusions going. Your mother never loved you. If she had, she would have at least pretended to believe, but she'd rather die than be around you. No one has ever loved you, and no one ever will. If there's any evidence that no God exists, all you have to do is look at your sad, pathetic life."

"N-n-n-nnnn." But she couldn't finish.

Christian smiled.

"Do what your mother was too scared to do. What your father should have done all those years ago when he realized you were just a stuttering little mutt."

Lucy shook her head.

Christian looked past her. "Do you see him? Right there in front of Luke? Do you see your daddy?"

Lucy turned around and stared.

"I can hear him, Lucy. Listen and you can, too." Christian swallowed and when he spoke, a strong southern drawl filled his voice. "They ripped up that Bible, didn't they? All because you cain't defend yourself. Ain't no way God's gonna show you a damned thing your whole life 'cause you cain't even defend yourself."

Lucy shook her head again.

"Get in that goddamn room and put that whip across your back! Maybe God can talk to ya, 'cause I cain't. I cain't do nothin' with ya no more. You're worthless." The drawl disappeared. "He's right, Lucy. He was always right. You are worthless, and you don't deserve to live any longer."

Christian watched as the mentally devastated woman raised the scalpel one last time. She stared at her father's ghost and brought the blade across her own neck.

Christian's head dropped back to the car as she collapsed. He didn't watch her black blood leaking out onto the pavement.

# EPILOGUES

# EXCERPT FROM THE ATLANTA
# JOURNAL CONSTITUTION

*The killer the media called "the Priest" committed suicide yesterday. The killer was a female named Lucy Speckle. Speckle had a long history of mental illness. She had been recently released from a halfway house after serving three years as an involuntary inpatient in a mental hospital. Records show she was remanded there after attacking occupants of a women's shelter for smoking cigarettes.*

*Speckle murdered at least four people, and based on early reports, she had plans to murder at least another four. In an elaborate plan, the FBI managed to determine Speckle's location. Once there, they began hostage negotiations. Agent Christian Windsor prevented Speckle from killing anyone else.*

*At the end of the standoff, Lucy Speckle committed suicide.*

*The FBI said in a brief press conference this morning that Speckle's motivation stemmed from an obsession with Agent Christian Windsor.*

*Two of the three FBI agents were severely wounded in the negotiation. Luke Titan and Windsor were transferred to Piedmont Hospital and both are expected to make full recoveries.*

*Luke Titan made headlines two years ago when...*

Christian's body still felt as if Lucy Speckle had just finished beating him. Sore didn't begin to describe the pain. He lay in his hospital bed wishing for death. He took the pills the doctors gave him. They both dulled the pain and made his mind hazy.

The pain relief was fine, but he didn't want his mind functioning at less than full capacity. He wanted to think, and so he never asked for more than they offered—never called the nurse saying he hurt too much.

Veronica and his mother refused to leave the hospital. They did give him space inside his room from time to time.

He enjoyed them being there, but he wished they would go home. They both were *allowed* to leave. Veronica had a concussion, but his mother was fine other than some tape burns on her wrists.

Getting help didn't take that long. With Lucy dead, Christian's mother was able to scoot across the ground and wiggle her way into Lucy's pockets. She found Luke's cellphone and dialed 911.

Christian had needed grafts on his chest. The skin there had thick yellow salve on it, and the nurses fed him antibiotics as if he were a burn victim.

"Hey," Luke said.

Christian's eyes had been closed, although he wasn't sleeping. He figured Luke knew it from his breathing patterns. Christian looked at the door and saw Luke sitting in a wheelchair. Bandages were wrapped around his head.

"You supposed to be moving around?" Christian asked.

"No."

"So why are you?"

"I wanted to check on you. How are you feeling?"

"Like someone savagely beat me with a whip and then skinned part of my chest."

"That makes sense," Luke said.

The two were silent and Luke wheeled himself in a few more feet. He turned and closed the door behind him.

"I saw your mother and Veronica on my way over."

"Yeah, they're refusing to leave."

"Veronica cares about you," Luke said.

"I guess so. I'm going to break it off with her."

"Because you think you can't protect her?"

"I know I can't," Christian said. He let his head sink into the pillow and closed his eyes.

"You've done a decent job so far. Two near-death experiences and she's survived both."

Christian said nothing. Veronica shouldn't have ever been in those situations.

"How are you feeling mentally?"

A minute passed as Christian thought about how to answer the question. He knew the answer. He had thought of little else besides his pain during the few days he'd been in the hospital. Yet, he didn't want to tell Luke about it.

He didn't know why he was feeling strangely similar to how he'd felt in the storage unit. Then, he hadn't wanted to talk about the apparition, and though he hadn't seen the Other since, apparently the feeling hadn't disappeared.

"I don't want to discuss it," he said finally.

"To anyone, or to me specifically?"

"You."

"Why?"

"I'm not sure."

"If there's anyone that won't judge you," Luke said, "it's me. I'm the one who pushed you, but it was necessary. I hope you see that."

"Was it?"

"If you hadn't, we would all be dead."

"Perhaps death is preferable to some things," Christian said.

"Perhaps."

Christian sighed. He didn't understand the feeling telling him to stay quiet about all of this, and he certainly wasn't going to his mansion looking for answers.

"What I felt when I spoke to her. It's not something I ever want to feel again."

"What was it?" Luke asked.

"Glee."

Luke was quiet for a second. He wheeled himself closer to the bed. "Is there anything wrong with taking glee in watching evil fall? Don't you think the allied powers felt glee when the Nazis finally surrendered? What about the people who tore down the statue of Saddam Hussein? Don't you think they were happy as they destroyed their dictator's legacy?"

"Maybe, but this wasn't a dictator falling. It was a mentally damaged individual."

"You think that Saddam Hussein didn't have as difficult a life as Lucy Speckle? It was different, to be sure, but the things he saw and was taught made him who he was. We're all shaped by our pasts."

Christian uttered a brief and nearly silent laugh. "Are you, Luke? Because no one knows about your past."

"Of course I am."

"Then tell me about that, and let's leave my mental state alone."

"Maybe I will tell you," Luke said. "I am what I am because of the things that happened to me. My point is that you can't feel you're different from those allied soldiers who cried tears of joy when news of Hitler's death got out."

"I don't agree."

"Which is fine. I think you will one day. Evil has to fall, or else, we would eventually all turn evil."

Christian said nothing and the two sat in silence for some time. Finally, Christian listened as Luke's wheelchair rolled from the room.

Before this all started, he had been so frightened of people leaving him. Of his partners moving on. His mother's eventual death. Even in the storage unit, he hadn't wanted to speak about the Other for fear that Veronica would leave him once she heard.

Now, Christian wanted everyone gone. He didn't want to look at any of them. He wanted to be alone, and if the rest of the world simply vanished, he'd be okay with it.

Christian drifted in and out of sleep for the next few hours. His dreams were black and he saw nothing inside them. They were desolate places.

Tommy came in at some point. Christian didn't know when. He saw his partner sitting in a corner chair when he woke. Christian looked around the room and saw his mother next to him, having pulled a chair up to his bed. He looked to the right and there was Veronica.

They both smiled at him.

"Hey, honey," his mother said.

Christian blinked and swallowed. "Water," he managed to say.

Veronica handed him a glass and he sipped through a straw, lubricating his throat enough to speak.

"I'm sorry I haven't been here as much," Tommy said as he stood. "I've been writing paperwork since the moment they let me out of this place. There's a lot to do, and I'm having to manipulate some of my memories to keep us from losing our jobs."

"I'm sorry," Christian said.

"All's well that ends well, I suppose."

"What's the press saying?"

"Well, you're the hero this time. You conducted the plan to find her and during the, um, *hostage negotiations*, Speckle committed suicide."

"That's better than the truth, I suppose."

"Much," Tommy said.

"Doc says you'll make a full recovery."

"With a bit of scarring."

"Stop being so damned negative," Veronica said. She was smiling but Christian couldn't force one to his own face.

"I'm going to stop by and see Luke. I think he'll have a scar, which I'm sure will dampen his spirits some, messing up that perfect head and all," Tommy said.

"I'm tired. I'm going to sleep some more." Christian knew how rude he sounded, but he didn't care.

"That's a good idea," his mother said.

"I'll be back tomorrow. Waverly gave me a new case.

Said if I was ready to do paperwork, then I was ready to capture criminals."

"That's kind of him."

The speaking stopped while Christian's mom and Veronica gave him very light hugs. They walked out of the room, though he knew they wouldn't be going far. Tommy stayed.

"I just wanted to say you did what you had to do, and I'm thankful for it. I know you didn't want to, and truth be told, part of me didn't want to see it. But you did, and I'm alive. So thank you."

Christian nodded but didn't tell him he was welcome.

Tommy returned the nod, then left the room.

---

Tommy said his goodbyes to Veronica and Mrs. Windsor, who insisted that he called her Patricia from now on. He headed down the white hallway to Luke's room.

Though he didn't know Christian was having a tough time shaking the things Luke had said, Tommy felt the same. He didn't like what Luke had done in that storage unit, but he couldn't place his finger on *why*. It had saved everyone's life, but it didn't sit right for some reason.

Christian's actions in his hospital room had said enough. He was in pain, without a doubt, but it almost felt like something *inside* him had died. Christian was a fragile person, still learning to cope with a reality that contained people other than his mother. Yet back in his hospital room, it seemed as if no one mattered. He had been cold, and not in the usual way, which had always been because he wasn't great at relating to people. He was cold as if his world had changed in some fundamental way.

Tommy didn't like it. He wasn't sure how to help Christian, but he knew in the coming months he'd do what he could.

He reached Luke's door and slowly opened it. There were two beds, but the curtain was drawn to the one on the far side. Luke was awake with a book propped in front of him.

"Whatcha reading?"

"The Rise and Fall of the Roman Empire," Luke said, looking up.

"Sounds riveting."

"It is. One of the author's premises is that Rome fell when they adopted Christianity, due to the fact that they stopped trying to conquer so many nations."

"I guess the author never met Lucy Speckle," Tommy said.

"No. He didn't."

Tommy stepped closer to the bed. "Going to have a scar?"

"Yes, they had to do some surgery to reconnect the bone where the crowbar hit me. I'm hopeful my hair will cover it."

"Let's pray it doesn't slow down your dating schedule," Tommy said.

"I've actually been thinking about starting to date. Outside of you and Christian, I don't have a lot of people in my life. It might be nice to have someone."

"It can be if it's the right someone."

Luke folded his book and put it on his lap. "You're upset with how I spoke to Christian, aren't you?"

Tommy nodded.

"Why?"

"I honestly don't know. It just didn't seem right. If you had done it to me, or anyone else in there, I don't think it would have mattered. But him? He's fragile."

Luke nodded and looked down at the book. "You're right, it wouldn't have mattered. I could have said the same things to you and everyone else, and none of you would have been able to do what he did. I had to push him, or we'd all be dead."

"I know. But what about now, Luke? What about the aftermath? Have you talked to him?"

"I have."

"Does he seem like the same Christian to you?"

"Do you think anyone is the same after something like that?" Luke asked.

"Don't bullshit me. Yeah, we'll probably all have bad dreams, but that's different than what he'll go through. He's changed, Luke."

"Yes. He's probably become the most efficient FBI agent in the entire force. I spoke to Waverly this morning. He said he's bumping Christian up a notch to Special Agent. So, if you think about it like that, I got him a promotion."

"I'm not thinking about it like that," Tommy said.

Luke looked up and Tommy saw something in his face that he'd never seen before. Luke looked like a human sculpture, etched in marble. Only his eyes showed any life, but the life there looked...alien.

"Thanks for coming by, Tommy. I'll see you at work."

# FOR CHRISTIAN WINDSOR

*For Christian Windsor*
  *Christian,*
  *This was a large turning point in your life, and you know that now. Our other partner is worried that you might not be able to come back from it, but I'm betting you will. Soon, very soon, I hope, we will be able to converse about my purpose. I didn't know that you would play such a major role, but it's clear now that you will.*
  *I believe in God, Christian. There is a being of such magnitude that it's tough to imagine in its full glory, but it exists. For sake of simplicity, we call it "him." I'm sure it doesn't care what we call it.*
  *God and I are at odds, and I truly believe that its angels are on my side. How could they not be?*
  *When you receive this letter, it will be too late for you to do anything, but take solace in knowing that you're on the side of the angels. You're on my side now.*

. . .

*Yours,*

> *Luke Titan, MD, Ph.D., Special Agent for the Federal Bureau of Investigations*

You're one step closer to reaching the end of the journey. Find out what happens next in *The Lover's Chain!*

# PREVIEW OF THE LOVER'S CHAIN

At least some part of Ted Hinson knew the difference between right and wrong, although he couldn't determine how large that part was. Two things were growing in him simultaneously: fear and confidence.

Neither had anything to do with right or wrong, but rather rationality and delusion. He felt fear because he was too intelligent to believe this could go on forever. Sooner or later, he *would* get caught.

Warring with the fear was an increasing sense of confidence because he hadn't been caught *yet,* which Ted Hinson's rational mind would call delusion.

Ted was thirty-eight years old and his reign of terror had begun two years ago.

While no single law enforcement entity knew it, five women had gone missing during this period at a precise clip of one every four months. It was now the twenty-fourth month in his reign, and time for another to disappear.

Ted decided on one woman every four months because of the *acclimation* process. It took four months to tame his lovers, or break them in, as one might a wild horse.

Sarah had been especially difficult and Ted was still trying to understand if it was her age, or simply her personality. She was pushing the limits of his patience, not to mention love, as well as his self-imposed four-month deadline. He thought that last night had been a major milestone in their relationship.

"You want to go to lunch with us?"

Ted looked up from his desk. Georgia Shingleton was at his office door. How long had she been standing there? His face showed no surprise, but he didn't like not knowing how long she'd been watching him.

"Not today. Have to catch up on some edits," he said.

"Okay. Want me to bring you anything back? We're heading to Raw Sushi."

"Mind bringing me a California Roll?"

"No, not at all," Georgia said. "See ya in a few."

"Thanks," Ted said and watched her leave. The California Roll wasn't for him, but for Sarah. He'd bring it to her as a thank you. Perhaps even as a peace offering.

Ted looked at his open office door. Had she been there long, and if so, what had she seen? Him staring mindlessly at his desk?

He needed to stop concentrating so hard, especially at work. Or rather, he needed to concentrate on *his work* while here and leave his lovers for home.

Ted turned to his computer screen and moved his mouse, causing the light to flare on.

He would deal with Sarah tonight. Hopefully, she would take the sushi with a bit of grace. If not, he might need to do something harsh—something he never wanted for any of his lovers—but her four-month acclimation period was at an end, and it was time to bring another into the stable. He didn't have any more time for Sarah's antics.

The trip was already planned for this weekend. Come Monday, Sarah would need to obey. Ted took the oath of marriage very seriously, and there would be no divorce. Not for him or any of his wives. If they chose to not love him, then...

*'til death us do part.*

———————

Sarah Yields was twenty-nine years old when her abduction occurred. Since then, she'd turned thirty, although she didn't know it. Not for sure, anyway. In the beginning, she had tried counting the days by counting her sleep cycles, but that was quickly lost.

Sarah spent a long time thinking about how it happened. She had been so stupid, and if she ever got out of here, she would scream it to the high heavens. She didn't care about victim shaming or any other terms she had been taught to despise in college.

Sarah had been foolish, and while that wasn't the only reason she was here, it was at least one of them. The other reason—and most important—was that "Ted" was fucking insane.

Sarah thought these things to herself, but she was

learning in perhaps the slowest and most painful way possible that she couldn't say them aloud.

Not if she wanted to avoid pain.

She'd been drinking entirely too much at a club and she had thought the man older, but intensely sexy. She'd quit listening to her friends' requests to come dance, and paid no attention to their protests about going home with the man she just met at the bar.

Alcohol and horny were a bad combination under normal circumstances, but when you combined those with a man named Ted, it turned into outright horror.

Sarah didn't remember much after leaving with Ted. She figured he must have slipped her a pill. When she woke, she was "at home," as Ted called it.

She sat in darkness. The other women here didn't talk. Sarah had spent many days trying to get them to. Ted's terror held them firm. They were all broken, just like he wanted. Sarah couldn't see the others in the darkness around her, but she heard them from time to time. Someone might let out a cry or a snore, depending on what they were doing.

Sometimes, a chain would rattle, the metal scraping across the concrete floor.

Sarah wasn't good with time anymore, but the women in the room seemed to share a sixth sense about when Ted returned. Their chains rattled more and Sarah found herself looking in the direction of the stairs. Light would shine down, and then a long shadow would be cast from the very top to where Sarah sat.

Ted's shadow. Her *husband*.

Last night had been bad. Sarah's tongue continually

went to the holes in her gums. They hurt like hell, but the blood flow had finally stopped at some point during the night. Sarah knew it was crazy, but when she'd spat her teeth out, she had placed them neatly by her side.

Three of them. She couldn't see them, but she knew they were there. If she ever left here, she'd still have them.

It was hard to hear much of what went on upstairs. Sometimes Sarah thought she only hallucinated the things she did hear. Sitting in the mostly silent darkness caused the mind to play tricks. Something else she had learned since meeting Ted.

The door at the top of the stairs swung open. Sarah squinted against the pain the light caused, but she didn't want to miss anything that came next. If she were to have any chance of escape, she had to be alert. She had to see everything she could.

The shadow grew in size as Ted walked down the stairs. They never squeaked under his weight. The entire basement was a huge slab of concrete, which also muffled any noise his harem might make.

"Here, love," he said.

Ted stood in front of her. Sarah knew better than to try and stand, plus her muscles couldn't take it today. Last night's beating hadn't knocked her out, but it had been the roughest yet.

Ted squatted and placed a small styrofoam box down in front of her. He opened it so that she could see inside.

"A California Roll. I wasn't sure what type of sushi you liked."

*I'm going to kill you. I'm going to kill you, and if I ever look at another sushi roll again, I'll kill whoever brings it to me,*

Sarah thought. She didn't say anything out loud. She simply pulled the styrofoam box back to her.

"Do you have anything to say?" Ted asked.

"Ssank oou," Sarah forced out, her swollen mouth not allowing her to form the sounds.

"You're welcome. I'm going away this weekend. Monday we'll have a new member of our family. I hope you'll treat her well, Sarah. I really do. I know how jealous you can be, and I know how mean that makes you. I hope you take some time this weekend to think about what you want out of our marriage."

*I'm going to kill you. I'm going to kill you. I'm going to fucking kill you.*

Sarah looked at the sushi, careful not to make eye contact while trying to see what was around her. It was always the same. There was nothing she could use to escape.

"Okay, then," Ted said.

He went through his ritual next. A disgusting thing that Sarah had learned well. He went from woman to woman, talking with each about his day. They never said anything in return.

He always kissed them and sometimes straight up made out, but so far he hadn't performed any hardcore sexual acts during *this* ritual. That came later, or at least Sarah assumed it did, although she hadn't yet been forced to take part.

Sarah listened to the psychopath talk to the other four women, speaking to them as if they were long-term lovers. He giggled, grew serious, petted them, and kept talking.

Finally, when he finished his rounds, he climbed those concrete stairs again and went to make dinner.

Sarah was lucky. He had brought her dinner early.

You're one step closer to reaching the end of the journey. Find out what happens next in The Lover's Chain!

# ON PURPOSE AND OTHER THINGS

Thanks for reading, and I mean that wholeheartedly. I love telling stories and without you, that wouldn't be possible.

I know at the end of books, a lot of writers offer you something free if you sign-up for their mailing list. What they're doing, essentially, is buying your email address.

I don't want to do that.

I think having a purpose in life is important. It adds clarity and meaning to what you do. I'm lucky to know mine and that purpose dictates my life: I'm here to tell stories. Nothing else even comes close to the happiness this job gives me.

With that said, if you like reading my novels and want to know when the next book comes out, sign-up below. No tricks. No buying your address. Just me telling stories and you enjoying them.

The way these relationships should work.

Join Here:
https://www.subscribepage.com/danielscott

# CONNECT WITH THE AUTHOR

Join Daniel's Email List here:

https://www.subscribepage.com/danielscott

# BOOKS BY DANIEL SCOTT

**Heinous Crimes Unit**

The Surgeon's Scalpel (Book 1)

The Priest's Fire (Book 2)

The Lover's Chain (Book 3)

Made in United States
North Haven, CT
16 February 2023